Rock Chick Reawakening

Also from Kristen Ashley

Law Man
Motorcycle Man

The **Fantasyland** Series:
Wildest Dreams
The Golden Dynasty
Fantastical
Broken Dove
Midnight Soul

The **Magdalene** Series:
The Will
Soaring

The **Three** Series:
Until the Sun Falls from the Sky
With Everything I Am
Wild and Free

The **Unfinished Hero** Series:
Knight
Creed
Raid
Deacon
Sebring

Other Titles by Kristen Ashley:
Fairytale Come Alive
Heaven and Hell
Lacybourne Manor
Lucky Stars
Mathilda, SuperWitch
Penmort Castle
Play It Safe
Sommersgate House
Three Wishes

Rock Chick Reawakening

A Rock Chick Novella

By Kristen Ashley

1001 Dark Nights

EVIL EYE
CONCEPTS

Rock Chick Reawakening
A Rock Chick Novella
By Kristen Ashley

1001 Dark Nights

Copyright 2017 Kristen Ashley
ISBN: 978-1-942299-76-9

Foreword: Copyright 2014 M. J. Rose

Published by Evil Eye Concepts, Incorporated

Acknowledgments from the Author

I would like to thank Liz Berry for being so danged excited when I said the words, "I'm thinking about doing Daisy and Marcus," when we were discussing what novella I could write for 1,001 Dark Nights. It gave me just the push I needed, with a little cheerleader high kick and jump to boot, to explore Daisy and Marcus and have the beauty I experienced while writing these pages.

And as ever, my gratitude to Erika Wynne, my sister in so many things, not just blood. She is always but always at my back, at my side or forging the way to cut a path to make things easier for me. It's impossible to express how exquisite it is to have that. But I try in each and every book I write to share just a little of the vastness of the beauty of the sisterhood that she gives to me.

Dedication

Last, this book is dedicated to all you Rock Chicks out there.
You know who you are.
You know the life you helped me build.
You know how much I appreciate it.
You wanted Daisy and Marcus, and it's my extreme pleasure to give them to you.
Rock on!

Sign up for the 1001 Dark Nights Newsletter
and be entered to win a Tiffany Key necklace.

There's a contest every month!

Go to www.1001DarkNights.com to subscribe.

As a bonus, all subscribers will receive a free
1001 Dark Nights story
The First Night
by Lexi Blake & M.J. Rose

One Thousand and One Dark Nights

Once upon a time, in the future…

*I was a student fascinated with stories and learning.
I studied philosophy, poetry, history, the occult, and
the art and science of love and magic. I had a vast
library at my father's home and collected thousands
of volumes of fantastic tales.*

*I learned all about ancient races and bygone
times. About myths and legends and dreams of all
people through the millennium. And the more I read
the stronger my imagination grew until I discovered
that I was able to travel into the stories… to actually
become part of them.*

*I wish I could say that I listened to my teacher
and respected my gift, as I ought to have. If I had, I
would not be telling you this tale now.
But I was foolhardy and confused, showing off
with bravery.*

*One afternoon, curious about the myth of the
Arabian Nights, I traveled back to ancient Persia to
see for myself if it was true that every day Shahryar
(Persian: شهريار, "king") married a new virgin, and then
sent yesterday's wife to be beheaded. It was written
and I had read, that by the time he met Scheherazade,
the vizier's daughter, he'd killed one thousand
women.*

Something went wrong with my efforts. I arrived in the midst of the story and somehow exchanged places with Scheherazade – a phenomena that had never occurred before and that still to this day, I cannot explain.

Now I am trapped in that ancient past. I have taken on Scheherazade's life and the only way I can protect myself and stay alive is to do what she did to protect herself and stay alive.

Every night the King calls for me and listens as I spin tales. And when the evening ends and dawn breaks, I stop at a point that leaves him breathless and yearning for more. And so the King spares my life for one more day, so that he might hear the rest of my dark tale.

As soon as I finish a story... I begin a new one... like the one that you, dear reader, have before you now.

Prologue

Building Castles
Daisy

"You're a lunatic!"

"You didn't think that when I had my mouth wrapped around your dick!"

"That's because you couldn't use it to talk!"

"Kiss my ass!"

"Not anymore, babe. We're done."

"Like I care."

"You'll care when you got no one's dick to suck to pay your cable bill."

My eyes were closed. I was lying alone in my dark room, on my back in my twin bed.

My bed was lumpy, seeing as Momma bought it from a yard sale, but I didn't feel that.

And my room was small and it didn't smell all that great, this coming mostly from the carpet. It smelled like that from all the way back when, when we first moved in. Momma didn't bother to do anything and got mad when I complained about it, so I'd tried to clean it myself, three times. But that smell just wouldn't go away.

I didn't smell the smell either.

And I could hear the words but even though they were coming from just down the hall, I was somewhere else.

I was building castles.

"Do not go there!"

"Fuck off."

"I'm tellin' you, *do not go there!*"

The door to my bedroom opened and so did my eyes, the beautiful castle I was building melting clean away.

I could smell the smell.

I could feel the lumps.

I could sense the closeness of the room, its thin walls, its fading, ripped-in-places wallpaper, the ceiling light I never turned on because the cover had been shattered on a night I didn't like to remember and now it made it too bright when I turned on the light.

"Daisy, sweetheart?" he called.

I looked to the door.

He was in shadows, those caused by the dark of my room and the hall. The only light was coming from somewhere else, probably her bedroom, because it was real late.

Tall, he had a beer belly but he also had broad shoulders.

I liked his shoulders. And his eyes. They were always twinkling when they looked at me. Even when he was mad at Momma, he'd look at me and it was like he forced the ugly out so all he'd ever give me was just the twinkle.

And he always used that soft voice when he talked to me.

Always, even when he was fighting with Momma, like just then.

"*Get away from that door!*" my mother screeched and I saw the shadowed man jolt as she shoved him to the side.

He came back, hand up, finger pointed in her face.

"Chill," he bit off.

I wanted to close my eyes but I didn't. I never could in times like these. Times like these, it was impossible to build castles. I knew this sure as certain.

Seeing as I'd tried.

His head swung back to me.

"I gotta go, girl. You need somethin', all you gotta—"

"She don't need shit!" my mother snapped.

His head turned to her again. He hesitated and I watched as his body moved when he took in a deep breath.

Then he looked back to me.

"I'm sorry, sweetheart," he whispered.

So was I.

I was young, only ten, but I understood why he was sorry.

But he wasn't sorrier than me.

"You tell *her* you're sorry. You treat me like garbage and you tell *her* you're sorry?" Momma shouted and the shadowed man jolted again because she'd shoved him again.

He reached in, grabbed the knob to my bedroom door, and pulled it to.

He did stuff like this too, a lot, because they fought, a lot. He tried to make it so I wouldn't see. Coming down the hall and closing my door. Or when they were in the middle of it and I was in the living room or kitchen, telling me quietly, "Maybe you should go to your room, sweetheart, and close that door, yeah?"

But he could never make it so I wouldn't hear.

With that, he disappeared.

But she didn't.

Her voice still came at me.

"That's it? You're just leaving?"

Nothing from him.

But more from her.

"You can't be serious. You cannot be freaking serious!"

He didn't reply.

"You're such an asshole. A total *freaking asshole.*"

He wasn't an asshole.

He was a good one.

The *only* good one.

Or, at least, the only good one I'd met.

He didn't hit her. He didn't hit me. Both of these my daddy did before he took off and we never saw him again. And other ones did besides (her and me).

He didn't steal her money (Daddy did that too). He didn't look at me in a way that made my skin feel funny (it was good that Daddy didn't do *that*). He didn't eat all the food in the house and drink all Momma's beer and bourbon and then complain there was never any food or beer or bourbon in the house and ride her behind until she got in her junker car and went out to get more for him (and yeah, Daddy had done that too).

Those kinds stayed around a lot longer than this one did.

Too long.

But never that long.

They always left.

Like Daddy did.

And I never missed them.

Yes, even Daddy.

But I'd miss this one with his twinkly eyes and his soft voice and the way he called me sweetheart not like that was what I was, but that was what he had. A sweet heart.

No, there were not a lot of those kinds. Not for Momma.

Not for me.

"*Stretch!*" she shrieked. "*You get back here, Stretch! Get back here!*"

The front door slammed.

"*Fucking motherfucker!*" Momma screamed.

I closed my eyes.

Let myself drift away.

And I started again to build my castle.

* * * *

"A Southern woman always has her table laid."

Miss Annamae was talking to me in her pretty dining room with the big dining room table all laid with the finest china, sparkling crystal, shining silver, and its big bunch of light-purply-blue hydrangeas with cream roses set in the middle.

She adjusted a napkin in its holder sitting on a plate that was sitting on a charger that was resting on a pressed linen tablecloth.

"If she's fortunate," Miss Annamae went on, and standing opposite the table to her, the fingers of my hands wrapped over the back of a tall chair, all ears, like I always was when I was with Miss Annamae, I watched her move around the table with difficulty. She wasn't a young woman. She also wasn't a beaten one, even losing both her kids and her husband and having to carry on alone. "She can change it with the seasons. I have Christmas china." Her faded blue eyes turned to me and a smile set the wrinkles in her face to shifting. "But you've seen that, haven't you, Miss Daisy?"

"Yes, ma'am."

And I had. Miss Annamae did her house up real pretty at Christmas. She always made sure I came over so she could show me all around and give me a tin of Christmas cookies she baked herself.

Momma had been working for Miss Annamae now for over two years. It was the longest job she'd ever had. She usually got fired a lot sooner than that.

I reckoned Miss Annamae kept her on as her daily girl not because she liked her or she did good work and kept a tidy house (which she did not, not Miss Annamae's and definitely not ours). I also didn't reckon she kept her on because she liked the fact Momma would be late a lot, show up hungover a lot, call off sick a lot, or one of her "men friends" would show at Miss Annamae's big, graceful mansion and cause a ruckus.

No, I didn't reckon any of this was why Miss Annamae kept her on.

I didn't know why Miss Annamae kept Momma on.

Except for the fact she was a good Southern woman.

Miss Annamae turned to the big window that faced her back garden, calling, "Come here, child."

I moved directly to her.

When I got there, she lifted her scrawny, veined hand to my shoulder and rested it there.

It felt light and warm.

"She works in her garden, a good Southern woman," she shared, her eyes still aimed out the window. "She cuts her own flowers, arranges them for her own table."

We didn't have any flowers at our house. It was actually good when the yard died during that drought last summer and became a big patch of dirt and scrub. It looked better not overgrown. Like someone lived there, they just didn't care. Instead of looking like no one lived there, and no one would ever want to.

The landlord didn't agree. He got up in Momma's face about it a lot. But she ignored him like she always ignored him when he got up in her face about things. Like the neighbors complaining about the fights or when she'd play her music too loud, which was also a lot, on all counts.

"You have sweet tea in your fridge, sugar, always," she said to me.

I nodded, looking from her colorful garden to her and feeling some pressure from her hand on my shoulder as she rested into me, giving me her weight.

I stood strong and took it. I'd take all her weight if she needed to give it to me. That's how much I liked Miss Annamae. And she had *all* my like seeing as Momma was how she was, her men were how they were, the kids at school were how they were, the teachers, the lady behind the counter at the store.

Everybody.

Yes, Miss Annamae had all my like mostly because there was no one else who'd let me give it to them.

This made it sad that Momma didn't let me come with her to Miss Annamae's house often, even though Miss Annamae always acted like she was real happy when I came. And I knew down deep in my heart this wasn't because I helped Momma and did all the gross stuff, like cleaning the toilets, so she could have a break from that kind of thing. But I did it a whole lot better than Momma did so Miss Annamae actually had the house kept the way she was paying to keep it.

Still, Momma didn't let me come often. Not even when I was in school and I had to walk home by myself and stay there by myself until she finished work (and then again stayed by myself when she went right back out).

I didn't know why this was either, except, even if it was mean to think, Momma didn't like it that Miss Annamae liked me.

I didn't understand this. If Momma was quiet and respectful, like Miss Annamae had told me a lady should be, a lot more people would like her.

I was beginning to think Momma didn't care if anyone liked her. So much, she'd rather they *didn't* like her so she didn't have to bother with people at all.

"No matter what you're in the middle of, a caller comes, you open your door to them, you invite them into your home, and you make certain they don't leave hungry," Miss Annamae carried on, taking my attention again.

Not easy to do in my house where Momma spent her money on smokes and booze and not so much on food for her kid.

I was looking forward to the day when I could get a job and I could have money and I could use it for whatever I wanted. I wasn't going to use it on smokes and booze, for certain. I wasn't going to use it on fancy dresses or shoes or handbags either.

I was going to keep my house like a good Southern woman would. My yard would be perfect. My house would be tidy. And there'd always be sweet tea and food in the fridge.

"Yes, ma'am," I said to Miss Annamae.

I felt her fingers curl on my shoulder and I was looking at her but I still felt sure as certain that her gaze grew sharper on me.

"A good Southern girl pays attention in school." She lifted her other hand to her temple then reached out and touched the middle of my forehead before she dropped it. "Ain't no call for a Southern woman to rub your nose in the fact she's smarter than you. But make no mistake, she's gonna be smarter than you."

I nodded.

She shifted closer and it felt like her eyes were burning into me.

"You find that time when you get yourself a boy, child, he holds the door for you. You enter a room before him. He closes you safe in his car. If you're at a restaurant, he gives you the seat with the best view. He stands when you stand. He offers you his hand when it's needed. And if you've got a touch with a drill and a hankerin' to use it, then you use it, girl. But if you don't and you got hooks you need put up in your bathroom, he best be gettin' on that for you and doin' it without any backtalk or delay."

"Yes, ma'am," I whispered, the wonders of such a boy as I'd never known making my insides feel funny.

"As for you, Miss Daisy, you take care of yourself," she continued. "Don't you leave the house without your hair set, your face done, and your earrings in." She patted my shoulder but then gripped again tight. "You get older, you'll find your style. And don't you let anyone tell you what that is. You're a good girl in a way I know you'll always be a good girl. Be proud of that. Good posture. Chin up. Show your pride, sugar. Be who you are however that evolves and don't let anyone cut you down."

Gosh, but it felt nice her saying I was a good girl.

It was harder to think of not letting anyone cut me down. That was always happening. I'd decided just to get used to it.

She let my shoulder go to put her hand in the pocket of the

pretty, flowered dress.

She pulled out a small, dark-blue box with a white bow.

I took in a hard, quick breath.

"And last, Miss Daisy, a good Southern woman always has her pearls," she said softly.

I looked from the box to Miss Annamae, but she was blurry seeing as I had tears in my eyes.

"Miss Annamae." My voice was croaky.

She lifted the box to me.

"Daisy, a gift is offered, you take it, you express your gratitude and later, you write a thank you note," she instructed.

I nodded, taking the box.

I pulled the bow but held it in my fist as I flipped open the top.

Inside, on a delicate gold chain, the prettiest, daintiest thing I'd ever seen, hung add-a-pearls. Their creamy gleam made me feel dazzled. The one in the middle was the biggest, getting a little bit smaller as they went down each side.

"One for every year of your life, child," Miss Annamae told me and I counted them.

She was right.

There were thirteen.

And I was thirteen.

That day.

It was my birthday.

"Now, to keep that set the way it should be, you come to me when you're fifteen and I'll add the next two pearls, balance it out," she shared.

My gaze drifted up to hers. "Miss Annamae," I repeated, my voice still sounding all choked.

And suddenly, with a swiftness I'd never seen her move, she was leaned into my face.

"You hide that from your momma. You hear Miss Annamae?"

I nodded, doing it fast.

I heard her.

Oh yes, I did.

"You wear those when the time's right. They're yours, Daisy. So you wear them when the time is right." She drew in a breath so big, I saw her draw it, before her voice got softer but no less strong.

"They're yours, child. However you need them when the time comes, they're yours."

I didn't understand what she meant by that but she was being so serious I felt it best to nod, and again do it fast.

"Thank you," I whispered.

The fierce went out of her face and she cocked her head to the side. Her soft, white hair swept back in the bun filtering with the sunlight coming in her window like she was an angel, she smiled as she lifted a hand and brushed my bangs sideways on my forehead.

"Every girl needs pretty things, every girl needs a little bit of sparkle however she can get it, but every *Southern* girl needs her pearls," she whispered back.

"*Daisy!*" Momma yelled from somewhere in the house.

I jumped.

Miss Annamae closed her eyes. Her wrinkles shifted again with her frown before she opened them, looked at me and said, talking quietly, "I'm sure your momma's got good in her, girl, but just to say, a Southern woman *does not* yell."

I nodded again.

She nodded back. "Go find your momma, child."

I stepped away, took another step, and started to turn.

But I stopped and turned back.

"Miss Annamae?"

"I'm right here, Daisy."

What did I say?

No.

How did I say *all* I wanted to say?

The words got caught, twisting, filling my throat.

"*Daisy!* Where are you?" Momma shouted.

"I know," Miss Annamae said, and from the look on her face I saw by some miracle she *did* know exactly what I needed to say without me having to say it. "Now go to your momma, child."

I nodded yet again, the feeling in my throat making wet pop out in my eyes.

I swallowed, took in a big breath, dashed my hand on my eyes and shoved the box into the pocket of my jeans.

Then I turned and walked slowly out of the dining room.

Like a lady.

* * * *

"I suppose you'll be wantin' some cake and ice cream or somethin'," Momma muttered when we were in her car on the way back home from Miss Annamae's house.

"No, Momma. It's okay."

"Now she's bein' that passive-aggressive bullshit," Momma kept muttering, now to herself, sort of. It was also to me.

I closed my mouth.

Momma didn't stop at the store.

In the end, I made myself bologna sandwiches for my birthday dinner while Momma got ready to go out to DuLane's Roadhouse.

But after she was gone, I ate my sandwiches sitting in front of the TV and I did it wearing pearls.

And three days later, Momma lost her job with Miss Annamae seeing as she went to work (late) and found Miss Annamae had passed quietly in the night while she was sleeping.

* * * *

I walked away from Quick Swap with the cash in my pocket.

I went right to the bus station.

I bought a ticket and sat outside on the bench, my two suitcases on the sidewalk by my boots.

The bus came.

The driver tossed my beat-up, second-hand suitcases under the bus and I climbed in.

There weren't a lot of folks there, which was good. I didn't feel in a friendly mood and Miss Annamae had taught me that a lady can make a stranger a friend in no time flat…and she *should*.

I picked a seat at the back by the window.

I rested my head against it and stared out, unseeing.

I heard the bus start up and felt it pull away from the curb.

When it did, I also felt the wet drip from my eye, rolling down my cheek. Then some more from the other eye.

I let myself have that. Just for a spell. Doing it, lifting my hand and touching my fingers to my neck where the pearls I'd worn every day for the last two years no longer were.

They were at Quick Swap.

The time had come when I needed them.

I knew Miss Annamae wouldn't mind. I understood her now. I understood a lot of things. Most of it I wished I didn't.

They were gone, all I had of her. She gave them to me on my thirteenth birthday and I'd pawned them on my nineteenth.

I'd miss them.

But not as much as I missed her.

When it was time to be done crying, I made myself be done. I opened my purse with its cracked fake leather and fished out my hankie (because Southern women carried hankies). I also pulled out my compact. I dabbed my eyes and carefully, swaying with the bus's movements in order not to make a mess of it (but I'd been doing it now for some time and I was good at it), I fixed my makeup.

I returned everything to my purse, kept it tucked in my lap, and looked down the long bus out the front window.

We were headed west.

It was going to be a long journey.

I rested my head back on the seat and closed my eyes.

Passing the time as the bus rolled over the miles, I built castles.

Chapter One

And Everything
Marcus

Marcus Sloan stood at the window in Smithie's office, staring down at the floor of the strip club, a quarter share of which he owned, but even so, he rarely came and he never did so when the business was in operation.

He didn't need to.

Smithie, who started the club, owned the rest of it and ran it, knew his business. He was serious about it. He was also honest. And he had the right reputation for the job—a man you didn't fuck with, but a man that took care of his business by taking care of his customers as well as his staff, from cleaning ladies to bouncers to bartenders to talent.

That was the first time Marcus had been there in over a year.

It was morning. Early. They didn't open until one. There were no windows to the building so the lights inside were on. Three women were moving through the space, one wiping down tables, the other two mopping the floor.

And two women were on the stage.

It appeared one was training the other.

The door behind him opened but Marcus didn't look from the window even as he heard Smithie walk in.

He kept his eyes on the stage.

"I hear you have a headliner," Marcus noted to the window, his attention aimed through it but locked on the blonde on that stage.

"Velvet rope, brother," Smithie replied and Marcus felt him move through the office.

He also felt him stop at Marcus's side.

"She danced with the other girls for about a week," Smithie told him. "Before I put her out there, saw it during her audition. Still had no idea how much of a stir she was gonna cause due to her talent. Don't need the bullshit it was gonna bring, all the boys shovin' their cash in Daisy's strings, the other girls get screwed since she's outshinin' 'em by a mile. If I clear the stage for her, she works the boys on her own, got no bitches workin' my nerves, whinin' about their tips. Four sets, three songs each, she gets her take and then some. The other girls get a good break to re-oil or whatever and the boys are primed and motivated to keep the goodness flowin' after she leaves the stage."

"Three sets, two songs, and no lap dances," Marcus stated.

"Say what?" Smithie asked.

Marcus turned to the man.

He was black. Big. In his day he'd been fit, never lean, a powerhouse. His body had gone somewhat soft with age, but Smithie hadn't gone soft. He was sharp, shrewd, educated, and street smart. His life had been bumpy, not as bumpy as some, but bumpier than most. He'd stood strong through it making smart decisions, wise alliances, and not many enemies.

"Three sets, two songs, and no lap dances," Marcus repeated.

Smithie's brows shot together as understanding came to him. "Thought we had an agreement."

They did.

Over a year ago, Smithie had hit some hard times with his family, one of his four women's brother finding trouble. He needed money to help him out. He'd taken it out of his business and to keep that business functioning, he needed a partner but would only take one who was silent, left the running of the club to Smithie, was open to a buyout when Smithie was back on his feet, kept his nose out of it, and simply took his cut every month.

The brother, with Smithie and his woman's help, found his way back to the straight and narrow.

And Marcus was more than likely going to be offered a buyout sometime soon.

But now, he was in.

"We did," he confirmed.

"Then, respect, Marcus, but I'm not sure where you're comin' from with that shit," Smithie remarked.

"An additional set and an additional song keeps the other girls off the stage," Marcus pointed out.

"Daisy's been headlining for five months, and so far, they got no problem with it."

"They'd have less of a problem if they had twelve more minutes on the stage to get tips."

"Sure they would but then Daisy'd be out and she'd be out a whack, man. Gotta have three bouncers go out right after she leaves the stage because a lot of 'em don't bother with shoving it in her string. They're in such a tizzy, they just throw those bills right on the stage."

"And the lap dances?" Marcus asked.

"It's double to get Daisy and they're only private. She doesn't work in the room."

"You got eyes on that?"

"Fuck yeah, Sloan," Smithie bit out, losing patience and not the kind of man who had trouble showing it, even to the kind of man Marcus was. "You've seen my setup. Got cameras everywhere. No one fucks with my girls."

"I don't want her doing lap dances."

"Man, a bad night, she could bring in five hundred, a thousand bucks on private dances. A good night, she's goin' home with two G's cash in her purse from lap dances alone."

Marcus looked back to the window, a feeling on the back of his neck like it was stinging just at the thought of that woman gyrating in some stranger's lap.

"You wanna explain this interest to me?" Smithie requested.

Marcus studied the headlining stripper at Smithie's.

Platinum hair and a lot of it. Petite frame, her ribs and waist trim to the point they were delicate, she also had slim hips and a narrow ass.

Her breasts were huge, however. Obviously augmented,

nevertheless, she'd clearly had them seen to by a genius. They somehow fit her frame, worked with the rest of her, drawing attention away from her height and her slight build, which could be seen as vulnerabilities, and giving her presence, potency, power.

But her face.

Her face was stunning. Wide smile. White teeth and a good deal of them. Big eyes. Elegant nose. Soft cheekbones. All of this she highlighted with the expert use of makeup from what was clearly a gift of superior genes into something that shone like a Hollywood starlet.

A starlet of a stripper who looked a good deal like Dolly Parton, who also likely got home the night before, earliest, three in the morning, and was right then, only hours later, back on the stage helping another girl by teaching her some moves.

"Marcus, brother," Smithie's voice came at him. "You got a problem with the way I do business, and I give you reason to have that problem, then we have a talk. I don't give you that reason, we don't have conversations like this one. That's our deal."

Marcus listened to him while he watched Daisy talking to the other girl and then she ran across the stage, doing it gracefully in platform sandals, her stone-washed jeans tight on her ass and hips and all the way down her legs. Still, after she ran the four steps, she launched herself high, grabbing on to the pole at least three feet higher than she was, her body swinging around by just her hands.

When the swing ended, she climbed up the pole, hand over hand. Doing this quickly, taking herself up another four feet, she flipped her bottom half over, wrapping her skinny legs around the pole. She dropped back, her hair flowing down, and with her only hold on the pole being her legs, she arched her back and slid down slowly, somehow circling the pole as she did it.

She ended this doing a layout with her hands on the floor, her legs in slow and controlled movements coming over her head one after the other. Her hands pushing off, she was up.

Standing straight with perfect posture.

And smiling like she hadn't moved an inch, much less just accomplished a feat of gymnastics—in a pair of tight jeans—that had to take a good deal of strength and effort.

Fuck.

That face.

That smile.

Fuck.

"I'm thinkin', watchin' that," Smithie kept at him, "you got a clue that every asshole who runs a club in Denver, Jefferson, Arapahoe, and Adams counties has been breathin' heavy down that girl's neck in hopes of recruitin' her. You think to take her off private dances and give her less time on the stage, she likes me. She likes the class of Smithie's most those other clubs don't have. She likes the other girls. She likes the velvet rope. She likes the Porsche she bought herself last month. What she ain't gonna like is that."

Marcus said nothing, watching her spot the other girl as she tried to do the same maneuver Daisy had.

And watching as the girl failed.

"And the other girls don't care, Marcus," Smithie kept at him. "She packs the place. Every night, gotta send men home from the line without them even getting in the door because the joint is jumping. That's cash in the cash register for you and me, brother. Cover is higher to get in with Daisy headlining. Bottles behind the bar getting empty and quick. My weekly order of booze has doubled. But it's also cash in the pocket not only of the dancers, but the bartenders and the waitresses. Everyone is happy."

Marcus turned his attention from Daisy to Smithie.

"Cut her back a set and a song each set and no private dances, Smithie."

Smithie became angry. "Been in this game seven years, Sloan. And those seven years, been waitin' for a talent just like Daisy to take Smithie's, and all the souls I got workin' for me who depend on it, to the next level."

"Increase her salary by half a million, give her four weeks' paid vacation, and cut her back a set and a song and *no private dances*, Smithie."

Smithie's eyes grew large.

"Half a mil?" he choked.

"I'll cover that."

Smithie's face got hard but his mouth moved.

"The other part of the deal is that I work to buy you out as soon as I can. I'm about two months from doin' that, now Daisy's here. I don't need you deeper, and no disrespect, I don't *want* you deeper. You knew that from the beginning too. I needed you and you stepped in for me and you got my gratitude for that. You got it from the heart," he thumped his chest, "*and* in the bank. But this is *my* club, brother, and I want it back."

"I'm not buying deeper in, Smithie, I'm covering the adjustment to Daisy's salary."

"And when I buy you out? Who covers Daisy then? I don't take a percentage of tips. Those are the girls'. I take a shave off the price of a lap dance of all the girls, but Daisy's elevated pricing goes to her. How do I cover half a million fuckin' dollars after you're gone?"

"You won't have to."

"How's that?"

"Because she'll be gone."

Smithie's brows shot up.

"*She'll—*" he started to explode.

He shut his mouth and stared at Marcus.

Then he whispered, "Motherfucker."

He wasn't calling Marcus that.

It was a muted exclamation.

Such was his shock, a surprisingly quiet one from Smithie, who was not a quiet man.

It took him a moment to compose himself and Marcus gave him that moment.

When he did, still quiet, he also seemed to brace, now surprising Marcus because it looked like he did it with a hint of fear, and Marcus had known Smithie for a long time and he'd never known the man to show fear.

"Don't go there," he said.

"I'm sorry?" Marcus asked.

Smithie shook his head. "Again, respect, brother, you got that from me, you know it, and I'm still askin' you not to go there."

There was the reason behind his fear.

Smithie might be a soft touch in some ways, but he was a hardass in all others.

But no one in Denver challenged Marcus Sloan.

Marcus turned fully to him.

Smithie took a small step back before he held his ground.

"Why would you ask that?" Marcus queried.

"She's a good girl."

Losing patience and having other things to do, Marcus crossed his arms on his chest, prompting, "And?" when Smithie said no more.

"She needs…" he started but didn't finish.

"She needs what?" Marcus pushed.

Smithie's focus sharpened on him.

"Peace."

Marcus felt that one word stab through his chest, feeling it and remembering the vision of a beautiful woman with lots of hair and a big smile, hiding the fact she had to be tired in order to help out a friend.

"Peace?" he whispered.

Smithie shook his head again. "She and me, we throw back a few. She's got time not dancin', I hang with her during some of it. Took her a bit. She don't trust easy. But she shared. And what she shared, Marcus, I'm askin' you, man, just don't go there."

Now Marcus was angry.

In fact, furious.

He did not show this outside the steely edge that was now in his voice.

"I would not harm a woman."

"Brother, you got a stable of whores."

"I do not," he clipped. "I oversee the management of a network of men who run escort agencies and I do this to make sure these men run this network appropriately."

"Like I said, you got a stable of whores. Or a *network* of 'em."

"You know that story, Smithie," Marcus said softly, the soft not gentle, just quiet.

And dangerous.

Smithie did know that story so he left that but didn't leave it alone.

"You got other shit you—" he started.

"Not your business."

"It is, you tie her up in it."

"She's not your business either."

Again, Smithie's eyes got big and he threw an arm toward the window. "She's a Smithie's girl and she's not my business?"

Marcus had had enough.

"Do you want a problem with me?" he asked.

"Of course I don't," Smithie spat.

"Then cut a set, cut a song in each set, no private dances and increase her salary, Smithie."

"Goddammit, Marcus," Smithie bit out.

"Do it," Marcus ordered then dropped his arms from his chest and moved toward the door.

He stopped and turned back when Smithie called his name.

"I won't have no problem havin' a problem with you if you make problems for her," Smithie declared. "Do you get that?"

They talked, Daisy and Smithie.

Smithie knew.

Peace.

Marcus nodded.

Smithie jerked up his chin in agitated anger and turned his back on Marcus.

Marcus walked out of the office, down the stairs, and through the club, not sparing Daisy a glance.

At that moment, he had business to deal with. He needed his head in that.

When it was time for Daisy, he wanted his attention fully on her.

But it would be time for Daisy.

Soon.

* * * *

Daisy

"Who's that tall, dark drink of handsome water?" I asked Ashlynn, my eyes on the tall man with broad shoulders and fabulous suit who was sauntering out of the club in the manner of a man who owned it.

In the manner of a man who owned anything he wanted.

"Don't go there," Ashlynn answered.

I looked to Ashlynn.

"What, sugar?"

She shook her head. "He's hot. Knew a girl who's had him and I'll repeat, he's *hot.* Took her out four times. All to fancy restaurants where she had to buy fancy dresses and shoes. And he gave it to her good at the end of the night, and I mean *real good*, the way she described it. He also, like, opened the car door for her and everything."

Opened the car door for her.

And *everything*.

Oh my.

"Ended it with her giving her a gold bracelet," Ashlynn carried on, recapturing my attention. "Pure class." Her look got intense as she stared into my eyes. "And he's trouble."

I glanced to the door that he'd obviously gone through because he'd disappeared, then back to Ashlynn.

"Trouble?"

Ashlynn didn't answer that question.

She just shook her head again and declared, "He wouldn't date a stripper anyway. Like I said. He's class."

I felt my mouth get tight.

I was not a big fan of judgment. I'd had that shit shoved down my throat from the time I could cipher. A mother like I'd had. A father like I'd had. The creeps, losers, and assholes my momma had no problem parading through her daughter's life, our home. The jobs Momma would get and lose and the reasons she'd lose them. The clothes I had to wear, bought at yard sales, garage sales, thrift shops. The crap people would say, not even worried I might hear. I didn't matter and my feelings sure didn't so they might not say it to my face, but they didn't do anything to shield me from it either.

I got out of that and it didn't get much better. Pretty much every bitch and dickhead felt they had a highly-tuned white-trash-o-meter and took one look at me, thinking it binged at the highest frequency.

Okay, so my momma wasn't all that. My daddy *really* wasn't all that.

But I'd gotten on a bus and left *all that* behind and never looked back.

Did that matter?

Hell no.

Yeah, so I'd found my own trouble in a variety of ways, mostly after Miss Annamae died, doing a stint at juvie that wasn't all that fun and learning my lesson.

And yeah, so I'd hooked up with some boys who weren't much to write home about, mostly because I liked boys, boys liked me, and a girl's gotta have a first kiss (and second, and third, etc.) and they were the only ones who asked me out.

They might not have been much, they might have been trouble, they might have treated me like crap, but at least they all (every one) were f-i-n-e, *fine*. I could pull in a looker like no other even before one of them bought me my boob job. It just sucked they were all also varying shades of asshole.

But I got my first job when I was sixteen and I was never late, never sick. I worked hard and showed respect that wasn't showed me, eating shit when I had to, pulling the knife out of my back and getting on with it whenever someone shoved one in there. I got my high school diploma. I might not have graduated with honors but I was on the AB honor roll every term.

No matter, they saw a woman with big hair and big hooters with a Southern drawl, a way with eyeliner and a penchant for rhinestones, and they thought they knew me through and through.

Sure, now I was a stripper.

And I'd been a cocktail waitress. A hotel maid. A grocery store clerk. And the hostess at a restaurant that, even though I'd been young, I still knew the majority of the clientele were scary individuals in the sense they were *feloniously* scary individuals. I knew I got that job and got paid good to do it because I had huge knockers and the ability to keep my trap locked shut.

What I was not and never had been was white trash.

Miss Annamae knew exactly what I was and she knew everything.

I could work a rhinestone, a lip liner, and a G-string, but I was a good girl where it mattered.

"He's also loaded," Ashlynn broke into my angry thoughts. "Men who got money like he does got the means to get themselves some that don't gotta shake it in guys' faces in order to make it."

"Well, if he's got a problem with seein' past that shit, sugar, then he might not want me even if he did expend the effort to look at me, which he did not, but I don't want me any of him, either."

Ashlynn looked like she let out a sigh of relief.

Whatever.

I turned my attention back to the door. "What's his name?"

"Daisy—"

I looked back at Ashlynn. "Don't wanna know it to go after him, honey bunch. Wanna know it to avoid him."

Ashlynn nodded. "His name is Marcus. Marcus Sloan."

Oh yeah.

That name said it all even if the suit and the hundred dollar haircut didn't.

He was class.

He was loaded.

He was trouble.

And I was a good girl.

So he'd been a good view for a few seconds.

And just like you always had to do in life, you took the good when you got it as you got it.

And when it was time for it to be done, you didn't hold on.

You moved on.

So I put Marcus Sloan out of my mind and I moved on.

Chapter Two

Nothing
Marcus

"Run the tape."

"Sir, Smithie says—"

For the first time in a very long time, Marcus Sloan's composure slipped.

"Run...*the goddamned tape*," Marcus ground out through his teeth.

The man in front of him sitting in the chair at a bank of monitors swallowed visibly, his eyes shifting only momentarily to the man at Marcus's back before he turned to the controls.

He hit some and all of the monitors blanked except one came up and the tape ran.

Marcus stood still and forced himself to watch.

It didn't last long.

He was not a man unaware that acts of lasting brutality could be delivered in shockingly short periods of time.

In fact, he'd built an empire on this.

He had just never seen anything like that.

The monitor cut out when the action on it had played out and the man turned it off.

But Marcus's eyes didn't leave it even when he asked, "Where's Smithie?"

"He's cut up about this, Mr. Sloan. Fired Milo 'cause he fucked up. Lost his mind when he did it. I was there. Thought he'd rip his head off. He—"

Marcus's gaze moved to the man.

"This was not the question I asked," he said slowly.

"He's...I think..." the man moved uncomfortably in his chair and said no more.

"I won't ask again," Marcus told him quietly.

"I...I heard someone say, uh...he and Lenny... That is, I heard they went to go see Shirleen Jackson and Darius Tucker."

Lenny, Marcus knew in keeping tabs, was one of Smithie's bouncers. Good kid, working his way through college providing security at a strip club. Marcus had met him once, and if he'd gotten a whiff of what he needed from the man, he'd have recruited him. But Smithie shared Lenny wanted to devote his life to finding a cure for cancer, something he'd lost a grandmother and aunt to, so he was studying biology in hopes one day to do that.

He might be studious but he was also a large, dark-skinned black man with a talent for security.

And if he'd seen what Marcus just saw, now he was a man with a mission that might put his future plans in jeopardy.

That did not factor to Marcus.

Only one thing factored.

And Shirleen Jackson and her nephew Darius Tucker, both colleagues of Marcus's, though they played different games on different turf, were a good start.

But only a start.

He turned on his foot and moved from the room, his man Brady following him.

Once they'd cleared it, they walked through the silent strip club, now closed when it should be open, lit only by its copious red neon.

When they were halfway to the front door, Marcus kept moving and didn't look to Brady even as he ordered, "I want a meeting with Lee Nightingale."

"Uh, sir?"

He stopped when they arrived at the door, his hand on the handle, and looked to Brady.

"Liam Nightingale. He's recently opened an investigations firm in LoDo. Get me a meet. Immediately."

"For what?" Brady asked.

"I'll explain that when I sit down with him," Marcus answered.

Brady got closer.

His man was tall, lean, cut, pretty-boy features, light-brown hair, all of this hiding his ability to get a variety of jobs done in a variety of creative ways. In other words, however he needed to do it to get it done.

He was uncomfortable, not with what he said next. Marcus had no problems with the people he trusted around him speaking their minds and Brady knew that.

He was uncomfortable with Marcus making any moves that might be unsafe.

This didn't happen often. In fact, it happened rarely and only when the need arose. But Brady was protective in more ways than it being part of his job description to protect his boss.

Marcus had bought that loyalty not with money but with something only men like him and Brady knew was much more precious.

"Mr. Sloan, we don't know dick about that guy."

"If you think that's true, you haven't been paying attention," Marcus told him, his tone not harsh, simply informative. "He hasn't been on the scene long but he's made quite an impact in the time he has."

"I've heard about him. I've heard he gets the job done. I've also heard his dad is a cop. Veteran. Years on the force. His brother is also a cop. So is his best friend, Chavez. And Chavez's younger brother, no one knows what that guy is. All they know is that Hector Chavez is a wild card and anyone with links to a wild card like that makes me uneasy."

"Nightingale's other best friend is Darius Tucker."

Brady gave a nod but said, "He's still untested."

"Then we're going to test him."

Brady held his gaze only a moment before he nodded.

Marcus continued to issue orders.

"You're on me, as usual. I want Louie on the streets. The other men stay on task. But keep Vince from this."

Brady's mouth got hard and he nodded.

Marcus's man Vince had his uses, they were valuable, but both

Marcus and Brady had had reservations for some time about the man.

Louie seemed able to keep him in check, however, so those valuable uses could be put to work without causing hassle or headache.

With no further words, they moved out of the club.

Brady opened the back door to the black sedan limousine that was waiting only feet from the entrance of Smithie's. Marcus folded in.

Brady closed the door, rounded the car, and sat in the front seat next to Marcus's driver, Ronald.

Through this, Marcus pulled out his phone.

He flipped it open and made the call.

"Yes, Mr. Sloan," his secretary Kelly answered.

"Smithie has a dancer. Her name is Daisy. Find out her address and send her a bouquet of daisies. A large one."

"Daisies?"

"Daisies. A lot of them."

"I'll do that right now, Mr. Sloan."

"Every day."

"Pardon?"

"Send her a bouquet every day. Starting today. Not the same color. But the same size."

"Right. Every day. Not the same color but large."

"Very large."

"Of course, Mr. Sloan. Anything else?" she asked.

"Not right now."

"Okay, then. I'll take care of it."

"Thank you, Kelly."

"My pleasure, Mr. Sloan."

He flipped his phone shut and drew a breath in through his nostrils.

He was trying unsuccessfully not to allow what he saw on that tape to run through his head.

As he was unsuccessful at this, he flipped his phone open again and made another call.

"Marcus," Shirleen Jackson answered.

"You or your nephew find him, you bring him to me."

There was a moment of silence before she replied, "That's not the deal we just made with Smithie."

"I'll handle Smithie."

"You got chops, Marcus, but the angry black man who just stormed outta my house is not a man I'm thinkin' even you can handle."

"They're close," he shared with her.

"Know that. He didn't say it but I think I got it. But that only makes it worse. Bottom line, she's a Smithie's girl and she got raped in his own goddamned parking lot. Doesn't matter to him she came back because she forgot something so he didn't know she was on the premises. Only matters to him that his shit-for-brains security guy left the cameras so his waitress girlfriend could give him a handjob in the handicapped bathroom stall. This means he was gettin' off when he should have been at his post, catchin' that shit and shuttin' it down so it didn't happen. Wasn't Smithie who got a handjob but he's takin' that all on his shoulders. He's feelin' a weight and that shit is heavy. So like I said, this is not a man who can be handled and I'm not thinkin' that's gonna change any time in, hmm…I don't know, say the next century."

"How many children does Smithie have, Shirleen?" Marcus asked.

"I can't keep tabs. Brother keeps addin' to his army," she muttered.

"Regardless, I'm sure they'd prefer him running his club and not serving twenty to life."

Shirleen had no comment to this.

"You find him, you bring him to me."

"Can we play with him first?" she requested.

"Be my guest."

"Marcus Sloan, always generous." She was again muttering then she ended it. "Later."

"Good-bye, Shirleen."

He flipped his phone shut and drew in another breath.

It was then he allowed himself to envision what was on that tape.

He was interrupted in this when Brady dropped the phone he had to his ear, turned his head, and looked into the back at Marcus.

"You have a meet with Nightingale at two," Brady told him.

In other words, in twenty minutes.

"Excellent," Marcus replied.

Brady turned forward.

Marcus breathed.

* * * *

Daisy

"Aren't these pretty?"

I didn't look.

I kept staring out the window of my apartment, seeing nothing.

"Daisy, hon," LaTeesha, one of Smithie's four women, got closer to me. (Yeah, he had four, and yeah, he worked that, and yeah, I got that—Smithie had that big of a heart, not one of them or not any of the gazillion kids he had felt what they got from him was lacking.)

"You're sweet, bein' here with me, sugar. But I'm feelin' the need for alone time."

"Daisy—"

I turned to look at her, my mouth open to say something, when I stopped and stared at the huge bouquet of flowers she held in her hands.

Daisies.

"Smithie?" I asked, still staring at the flowers.

"Marcus Sloan."

My eyes shot to hers.

"Uh...pardon?"

She smiled gently. "They're from Marcus Sloan."

"Marcus Sloan?"

She misunderstood me, thinking I didn't know who he was when I didn't. Not really. But I'd heard of him. And, of course, seen him at the club since I noticed he'd come in every once in a while after that first time I'd seen him with Ashlynn.

"He's Smithie's partner. Silent partner." She said that last quickly, and I knew the way it came at me the "silent" part was *very* silent. "He...he's..." She seemed to struggle before she went on, "A good man. Kind-hearted. He helped me and Smithie with some things once and I'm grateful he did. Don't know what we would've done if he hadn't. My guess is that he heard what happened and—"

Oh no.

Nononononono.

No.

My chest closed up so I had to force out my, "Please."

She set the daisies aside and crouched down beside me, taking my hand.

The instant she touched me, I pulled my hand free.

"Darlin' child," she whispered, the words broken, like she was going to cry.

"I need some alone time," I whispered back.

"Okay, baby, then you go into your room and I'll stay right here so if you find you're not feelin' the alone, I'm real close so you don't gotta be."

"Thank you but by alone, honey, I mean *alone*."

She scooted closer in her crouch and her voice dipped low and even sweeter.

"Hon, I know you think you know what you want right now but you don't. You need me here. And I'm gonna stay here, Daisy. You need to be alone, I'll give you that how I can. You wanna be in here, I'll go to the kitchen. You wanna lie down in your room, I'll be out here. But I'm not leaving."

The tears hit my eyes and they stung.

I looked to the window, and to control the tears, my tone was ugly when I rapped out, "Do whatever you wanna do."

"Daisy?"

"What?" I snapped.

"I could turn back time, I would, baby."

She said that like she *really* meant it.

I looked back to her and hissed, "That makes two of us."

She bit her lip, wet trembling against her bottom lashes, and nodded.

I again looked out the window.

I felt her presence leave me but it didn't leave my apartment.

And I stared out the window knowing I was done.

My daddy beat me. Then he left us with just what he gave us

when he was with us. Nothing. My momma gave not one shit about me. Every man I'd had in my life (outside Smithie, and long ago, a man I barely remembered, just his shoulders, his eyes, and his name, Stretch), had treated me like trash.

And I was finally getting it.

Finally.

They treated me like trash because that was what I was.

The kind of girl some loser you once gave a lap dance to who was ejected because the motherfucker was way too fucking handsy jumps you in a parking lot, lands his fist in your face until you can't think straight, and violates you on asphalt.

I didn't move from that chair not because it was comfortable.

I didn't because it hurt too much to move and I'd already learned that there was nothing, sitting or lying down, that felt good on my scraped-raw back and ass.

Yeah.

That's where trash belonged.

Thrown to the asphalt just like what it meant.

Nothing.

Miss Annamae had been wrong.

Everyone else had been right.

I got treated all my life like I'd been treated because that's who I was.

I wasn't even trash.

I was nothing.

And coming to this understanding, I stared out the window not seeing anything and I didn't even try to build castles in my head. I didn't surround myself with a moat, heavy doors solidly bolted to keep the bad away, knights in armor always close to protect me, pennants flying to the glory that was me. The princess high atop a turret in a stronghold, a glorious, magnificent, grand castle made of impenetrable stone, safe and protected where no one could hurt her with words or fists or anything.

You didn't keep trash safe.

You threw it away.

But nothing?

Nothing was just...

Nothing.

* * * *

I woke when I was lifted and immediately started struggling no matter the pain—throbbing in places, acute in others—that tore through me.

"Shh, darlin', quiet now, it's only me."

I went slack in Smithie's arms.

He carried me to my bed. LaTeesha was already there, folding back the covers.

She straightened and turned to Smithie and me as Smithie bent and laid me out on my sheets.

"You want me to help get you in your jammies?" LaTeesha asked gently.

In answer, I turned my back on her.

I heard her sigh.

I felt Smithie pull the covers up over me.

He tucked them lightly around me and then I felt his lips touch my temple.

I pressed my head into the pillows to get away.

"Baby girl—" he started to whisper in my ear.

"Not now, honey," LaTeesha advised her man. "Not now."

"Fuck," he murmured as I felt him move away.

The light went out.

I didn't hear the door close and I reckoned this was because one of them came back. I heard a muted sound like they'd put a very full glass of water on the nightstand.

Only then did I hear the door close.

So only then did I feel it was safe to turn carefully, doing this to my belly so I didn't rest any weight on my scrapes, and I looked through the dark.

There was a shadowed bouquet of daisies on my nightstand.

I stared at them and I did it focusing only on the darkened shapes of the blooms until my eyes closed and I fell asleep.

* * * *

And when I woke up hours later, those daisies were the first thing I saw.

* * * *

And as the days passed, every one, there came a huge bouquet of daisies.

I went to bed wandering through an apartment filling up with brightness.

And I went to bed with the scent of flowers in the room, the sight of shadowed petals the last thing I saw.

And that bright, hopeful, happy beauty was the first thing that hit me every morning.

Chapter Three

Snow White
Daisy

"What happened to your face?"

I looked to the kid standing beside me where I sat on the bench in Washington Park, a place I'd gone to escape my apartment, my thoughts, my life.

And those daisies.

Even I couldn't feel like shit in a house filled with daisies.

I didn't think of daisies.

I looked at a kid who was young, in his early teens, maybe even younger than that, Hispanic and already a very good-looking boy. He had another boy with him, black, gangly. I could see the other one would be tall and he wasn't yet growing into what he'd become, but the promise of it was there. He was standing further away, shadowed by the shade of a tree, not bold enough to approach, so I turned my attention back to the one who'd gotten close.

"It's not polite to ask a question like that, sugar," I told him.

"I hope you fucked him up right back," he said and I wished I was able to share that I had.

I looked closer at him.

"Fuck, you didn't get the shot at fuckin' him up," the kid muttered, his face turning hard, and my attention grew sharper.

When it did, I noted he needed a shower. A haircut. A change of clothes.

Food.

And he saw things others wouldn't see.

Primarily, whatever my face had told him that other kids his age would never have seen. Hell, even most adults wouldn't have read it on me.

Damn, he was a runaway.

I cocked my head. "When's the last time you had somethin' to eat, boy? And by the way, kid your age shouldn't say fuck. *Comprende?*"

His face got even harder before his eyes darted beyond me, his body grew tight, and his friend said urgently, "P, let's go."

He didn't delay. They both took off and vanished quickly, even in an open park on a sunny day.

It was then the sun was blocked from hitting me and I turned my attention swiftly that way, bracing, preparing to launch myself from the bench and run if I had to.

I stayed still as I saw Marcus Sloan standing there in another impeccable suit, hands in his trouser pockets, eyes cast down to me.

"Daisy," he murmured.

Please, God, let this not be happening.

My face was still a mess, as evidenced by that kid coming up and mentioning it to me.

And I was...

Well...

Me.

"Mr. Sloan."

"Marcus," he corrected me.

Okay, this was happening.

I lifted my chin a little and kept it there but said nothing.

He had sunglasses on, smoky ones that were handsome on him and probably cost a mint.

Headlining Smithie's I could afford glasses like those (well not those, those were for a man, but the like for girls).

Years of scraping by, I'd made it.

Stripping.

Smithie was giving me paid leave. I was going back as soon as the bruising was out of my face and the scabs were gone from my body.

I was doing this because I had a Porsche to pay for, for one. And what did it matter what I did, for another. I got paid a load dancing around for schmucks with hard-ons. No reason not to keep doing it.

And yeah, not even after what had happened to me. I knew without a doubt that wasn't why I'd had some asshole rape me. Assholes did that kind of shit to women no matter what she did for a living, mostly because they were *assholes*.

Still, even behind his shades, I knew Marcus Sloan was studying me.

I didn't like it but Miss Annamae's training kicked in and I said, "Thank you for the flowers."

He inclined his head but said nothing.

"They're real nice but you can stop sending them," I told him.

He still said nothing.

Whatever.

I looked around our area of the park and back at him.

"You take a stroll through Wash Park often?" I asked.

He spoke then.

"I'd like to take you out to dinner tonight."

I stared up at him, not wearing any sunglasses, so my expression was probably not hard to read. Even if I'd had them on, my mouth dropping open would have given me away.

I snapped it shut and straightened my back. This caused only a hint of pain as the tightness of the scabs reminded me they were there.

"Thank you, but you've made your point with the flowers. And you have nothing to worry about. I'm coming back to work and I'm not blaming anyone for what happened, except the asshole who did it to me."

He nodded but even doing it, he said, "With that, I'm afraid it's clear that I haven't made my point with the flowers."

What?

"What I'm trying to say, Mr. Sloan—" I began to explain.

"Marcus."

"Marcus," I snapped and watched his very fine lips twitch.

Whatever.

I carried on.

"You and Smithie will have no problems from me."

"I didn't suspect we would."

"Good," I returned. "So thank you for..." I lifted a hand and flitted it through the air, watching his shades move to it and stay locked on it in a way that made me feel funny, "your kindness, but there's no need to take it further."

When I dropped my hand to my lap, he rocked back on his heels, his shades returning to me.

He didn't say anything for a long time, he just looked at me, and I fought squirming.

Finally, he spoke.

And when he did it, his deep voice wrapped around the words warmly, communicating that warmth to me.

"Daisy, I'd very much like to take you to dinner."

"Thanks," I returned sharply, using my tone to fight back that funny feeling that just kept growing. "But no thanks. I don't need a pity date, not to mention..." I lifted my hand again, this time to gesture stiltedly to my face, "I'm not feelin' good about goin' to some fancy place and bein' on show."

"I don't pity you," he told me.

"Really?" I asked, cocking my head again, feeling my hair move and seeing his head shift slightly so I knew he watched it. "A girl who got the skin scraped off her ass in a parking lot because some guy tore her clothes off, threw her to the blacktop, and banged the shit outta her when she was only kinda conscious?" I righted my head and nodded. "Right. I get it. You don't pity *that* kind of girl. *My* kind. I work a pole, I got it comin'."

I stopped talking, but I'd done it so heatedly, I'd stupidly not paid close attention to him while I was doing it.

So when I stopped talking, I had no choice but to pay attention because the entirety of Marcus Sloan had changed. Every inch. Every *molecule*. The change filled the air and circled around me, drawing me into its snare like I was Snow White reaching for the apple, even knowing the dangers that lurked if I took a bite.

"I misspoke," he whispered, his words slithering over my skin, not like a snake.

Like silk.

And they kept doing it as he kept speaking.

"I don't pity you. I'm very sorry for what happened to you. What you endured. *Very* sorry, Daisy. However, I don't wish to have dinner with you because I pity you. I wish to have dinner with you because you're the most beautiful woman I've ever seen."

Yep.

My mouth dropped open at that too.

"It's too soon for you," he murmured. "I apologize. We'll take this slow. To that end, I'd be honored if you'd have lunch with me on Friday. Somewhere quiet where you won't feel on show."

"It's Wednesday," I told him something he likely knew, but it being Wednesday, no way my face would be okay to go to lunch anywhere by Friday.

Not at all.

Definitely not with a man like him.

And taking it slow meant *taking it slow*. Friday was only two days away. That wasn't slow!

"Yes," he agreed.

"I…you…uh…"

I stopped talking.

"Friday," he decreed.

"No," I whispered.

He seemed to lean toward me.

At that perceived movement, I scrambled off the bench and took a big step back.

His hands came out of his pockets and he lifted them to his sides.

"Daisy, I won't—"

"No," I shook my head. "No more flowers. No lunch on Friday."

"Please, I simply—"

"No."

It came out strangled.

Then I turned and ran.

But I heard him order curtly, obviously not to me, "Make sure she gets home safely."

And whoever it was did just that if the Mercedes trailing me in my Porsche was anything to go by.

Crap.

Damn.

Shit.

I stood at the window in my apartment staring down at the Mercedes that didn't move from sitting at the curb in front of my building.

Crap.

Damn.

Shit.

Okay.

Whatever.

Shit happened. Then it stopped happening and you moved on.

Whatever this was with Marcus Sloan would stop happening too. And I'd move on.

I turned away from my window.

And all I saw was daisies.

* * * *

"I'm likin' it but it needs some sparkle," I told Chardonnay late Friday morning while sitting in the dancer's dressing room at Smithie's as she modeled her new stripper duds for me, doing it busting some moves.

It was pasties, a G-string, and platform stripper sandals.

She still needed sparkle.

"Daisy, where am I gonna put sparkle?" she asked, staring down at her mostly nude body.

"Glue gun the shit outta some and put it over your coochie, girl," I advised. "Boys' eyes go there, least that's covered and they're not lookin' at your tits. Well, at least not all the time."

"This bears contemplation," Chardonnay murmured.

This bears contemplation.

This bitch slayed me.

Her name wasn't Chardonnay. It was Penelope. She was premed, a senior, already accepted to medical school. She was also the shit because pretty much everyone knew she was stripping and she didn't give a crap.

"By the time I'm practicing rheumatology," she'd shared with me, "I'll be getting paid a whack and it'll be all mine. I'll buy myself a BMW and a big house in Cherry Hills and I'll do it right off the bat because I won't have student loans. So they can think what they want. They can also kiss my ass."

I, obviously, could not fault this way of thinking.

"Black on black, but also some silver," I advised. "Subtle but packs a punch."

"I'm not sure my powers with a glue gun are up to scratch," she replied.

"Take it off. Rinse it out and give that bitch to me," I told her. "I'm hell on wheels with a glue gun and I'll set you up."

She grinned at me as a knock came at the door.

I looked that way as Chardonnay called, "Just a minute." Her next was, "Okay, decent." And I turned to her and saw she'd thrown on a robe.

I also saw she was staring at the door with big eyes and lips parted.

I looked again to the door and then I had big eyes and parted lips.

Oh hell.

Marcus Sloan dipped his chin to Chardonnay and looked to me.

"Daisy, may I have a word?" he asked.

No, he could not.

"I'll just—" Chardonnay started.

"You can stay here," Marcus told her. "Daisy and I'll go to Smithie's office."

No, we would not.

"I don't think—" I began.

I got no more out because his eyes came to me.

He'd never looked at me without sunglasses on.

He had blue eyes.

They were gorgeous.

They were also more.

Those eyes had seen many things. Not a lot of them good. And quite a number of those not-good things were *very* bad.

I got that. Boy did I get that.

But there was even more.

Another person might find his eyes frightening, that seen it all and didn't give a shit about any of it look that wasn't cold and impersonal, just cynical and sly.

I did not find it frightening.

I found it captivating.

He took a step into the room but lifted his arm to the side to indicate the door and said in an invitation that wasn't exactly that, it was more a command, "Daisy."

There was something about the mix of his gentlemanly manner and his commanding tone (and, let's face it, presence) that made me lift my ass off the chair I was sitting on and move his way.

He was not an obstacle to getting out the door so he didn't move.

However, he *did* move after I cleared it because he followed me.

Then he put his hand light on the small of my back.

No pressure. Just a touch.

Even at "just a touch," I felt my shoulders get tight. But I didn't want to expose my reaction, give him something to read about me, make him think I was afraid or protecting myself, especially after what he knew happened to me and the fool I'd made of myself at Wash Park.

And as we walked down the hall, into the club, and toward the stairs that led up to Smithie's office, my tension at being touched became something else as the feel of the touch penetrated.

He wasn't pushing me. He wasn't guiding me.

He was a gentleman walking a lady through a strip club the way a gentleman should, regardless it was a strip club in which she was a stripper.

I started feeling funny again.

His touch left me as we climbed the stairs and I was embarrassingly aware that I was still slightly stiff from what had happened to me, not to mention my ass might be in line with his eyes.

I motored right through that and stopped at the top landing outside the door, looking down as he climbed the last two steps.

He put his hand right to the handle and murmured, "Smithie isn't here."

He pushed the door open but didn't move.

He waited there and did it with his eyes on me.

It was then I realized he wanted me to go in before him.

He'd opened the door.

For me.

I started feeling funnier and quickly walked into the office.

I didn't go far, stopping in the middle and turning to him.

He didn't go far either, but oddly, he stepped away from the door and moved across the space.

In other words, he wasn't barring me in. If I wanted to leave, I had a straight shot. He wasn't in my way.

Oh my.

"We have plans."

I focused on him and not my thoughts.

"Pardon?"

"Lunch. Today. You. And me. We have plans." The words were short. Impatient. But even so, not unkind.

I didn't know how he pulled that off but I didn't put too much thought into it.

I had to get this done. He was my boss (kind of). He was also an important man. I didn't know that outside of the fact I *knew* that and I couldn't forget it for a second.

So if he wanted "a word," I had to give it to him.

And then get away.

"No we don't."

"Our last meeting didn't go as I'd hoped but I had thought I'd made my intentions clear," he replied.

I didn't know how to respond to that because he had, I just didn't get it nor did I want it.

All of a sudden, a change came over him, and even though it softened his features, warmed the cynicism clean out of his eyes, I still felt the tension in my shoulders increase.

"Are you okay?" he asked quietly.

"Uh, yeah," I answered normally.

For some reason he looked to the floor, beyond me, then again to me.

"You're here." Now his voice wasn't quiet, it was soft with inquiry and concern.

Here.

Where, out back, I'd been raped just over a week ago.

God, I needed to get away from this man.

"Yeah," I agreed. "I'm here."

"Should you be?"

"Chardonnay had a wardrobe question," I explained.

And again his expression changed. This time it didn't hide he thought I had a screw loose.

"I'm sorry?"

"Chardonnay. She had a wardrobe question," I repeated. "And her roommates are bitches. Totally judgey about the stripper thing so she couldn't model at her place because she has to show me her moves in her new getup and they're there. She couldn't come to mine. So we're here."

"Why couldn't she come to yours?"

I couldn't tell him that. I couldn't tell him it was because the place was filled with daisies and I didn't want to answer the questions that might bring. I didn't want to tell Chardonnay or anyone not only where those daisies were coming from but that, in my worst moments, their bright, happy beauty was the only thing that was seeing me through.

So I didn't say anything.

"Does she know what happened to you?" he asked gently.

I nodded.

His mouth grew hard, and probably because of that, his words were terse. "She should be more sensitive."

"I'm okay, Mr.—"

"Marcus," he clipped.

"Right. Marcus. Sorry," I muttered.

"Smithie isn't here," he informed me.

He'd already shared this intel so I didn't know why he was repeating this to me.

"Okay," I replied.

"This means you're not here for any reason unless Smithie or Lenny are here, and if you need to be here and neither of them is available to be with you at all times, you call me. I'll put a man on you."

At all times?

He'd put a man on me?

I stared at him.

He reached into the pocket inside his suit jacket, took out a silver card case, flipped it open, and extracted a card. He flipped it shut, returned it, and walked to me, stopping not close (thankfully).

He held the card up between us, offering it to me with two fingers extended.

Lord, this man was fine. Even offering a business card!

"I don't...I don't..." I swallowed, ignoring the card, "need a man on me."

His eyes turned hard too, and at their glinting fury, I finally started to be scared of him.

I fought taking a step back.

"They haven't found him," he whispered.

"I know that," I whispered back.

And that made me shiver.

I wasn't thinking about that. The fact the guy who violated me got away.

Smithie said he was taking care of it. Detective Jimmy Marker, who talked to me at the hospital when the staff called the cops after the ambulance took me there, said he'd do everything in his power to find him.

I was thinking only about that.

"You need be safe. So you're going to be safe," he decreed, lifting the card up higher between us.

"You need to stop sendin' me flowers," I didn't exactly decree because my voice was kind of shaky, but I hoped he'd get my message.

"I will, if you go to lunch with me tomorrow."

"You need to stop asking me to lunch."

"Fine. Then go with me to dinner tomorrow."

"Mr. Sloan—"

He leaned into me, his face close, I could smell his expensive cologne, and I snapped my mouth shut.

"Marcus," he whispered.

"Okay," I breathed.

"Dinner tomorrow."

"No."

He ignored me.

"I'll pick you up at seven. You won't be on show. But you will be safe from anything you perceive might make you unsafe, including me. I simply want your company at dinner. That's all, Daisy."

"Please, stop doing this."

His brows went up. "Why?"

"You have to ask?"

"Daisy," he said gently, reaching to me, grabbing my hand and pressing the card in my palm. Closing my fingers around it, he continued to hold me lightly and I didn't pull away because I didn't want to share what that would expose either. "You were harmed. You were hurt. But what happened to you didn't make you stop being who you are or make it so you shouldn't live your life and enjoy doing it."

"I'm not talking about that."

"All right, so explain to me what you're talking about."

"I don't feel like it."

He nodded once. "Fine, so explain it to me over dinner tomorrow night."

"Marcus—"

"I'm not going to give up."

This was beginning to make me mad so I shared crankily, "Well, that doesn't make me feel real peachy."

His fine lips twitched and he asked, "Do you not find me attractive?"

Was he *crazy?*

"Of course I find you attractive. You're all—"

I cut myself off then because I wasn't paying attention to what I was saying, mostly the fact I shouldn't be saying it.

Those fine lips of his curled up.

Oh Lord.

"I'm all what?" he pushed.

"Can you let me go?" I snapped.

To my shock, he let me go, and not only that, he took a step back.

You will be safe from anything you perceive might make you unsafe, including me.

I started breathing funny.

"Would you like me to explain why I don't wish to give up?" he asked.

Hell no.

"No," I answered.

He let that slide and told me, "I want to be clear. I don't want to come on strong."

"Well, you're failin'," I shared.

At that, he smiled.

I felt my throat close.

With that smile, the cynicism and sly went right out of his eyes.

They were twinkling at me.

Twinkling at me.

"You mistake me," he said softly. "I don't want to come on strong. I don't want to take this at a pace you aren't comfortable with. Not with what happened to you, but you should understand, I wouldn't do that even if that hadn't happened to you. So you'll set the pace. Just as long as there *is* a pace."

"And if *I* don't want there to be *a pace?*" I asked.

"Then I'd like the courtesy of you sharing why you wouldn't."

"And I'd like the courtesy of you not makin' me do that," I shot back.

He studied me a second then looked beyond me.

Again, he changed and he did it taking another step away from me, his face closing off so much, the cynicism and sly didn't even come back.

He gave me nothing.

"I see," he murmured.

I shouldn't ask.

I really shouldn't ask.

I asked.

"You see what?"

"You know who I am."

"Yeah. You're Marcus Sloan."

He shook his head. "That's not what I mean and I believe you understand that."

I did, right then.

And what I understood made me laugh.

It just poured out of me.

And I guessed I really needed to laugh because I did it so hard, I bent over with it, wrapping my arms around my belly.

When I got myself together, still giggling, I straightened, lifted a hand to my eye and swept it across the wet under it, hoping my hilarity didn't mess up my makeup seeing as I'd had to wring miracles to conceal the fading bruises that morning.

"That's funny," I told him unnecessarily.

He didn't find anything funny. He still looked closed off but also there was a hint of transfixed that I didn't get.

"Your laugh sounds like bells," he whispered.

I immediately stopped giggling.

He visibly pulled himself together and kept talking.

"Even so, I'm not certain what was funny."

"You," I shared.

"Me?" he asked.

"You, thinkin' I'd have a problem with you bein' Marcus Sloan," I expanded.

"Do you know who I am?"

"Nope." I shrugged. "Don't care either. Though, that's to say 'nope' don't mean that I don't know. I just don't really *know*. I still don't care. And that's not why I don't wanna have dinner with you."

"I'm still not understanding."

"Honey bunch, I'm a stripper."

"Yes. And?"

I shut up.

Dear God, he thought I thought I was better than him.

No.

He thought *I* thought I had reason to think I was better than him.

"I don't judge," I said quietly. "Life's life and a person's gotta do what they feel they gotta do to get along in it."

"This is correct."

"So I don't care what you do or who you are."

"And this delights me."

My heart started racing because it did. It *delighted* him.

And I knew this because his eyes were again twinkling.

"Men are assholes," I shared.

"Some of them are, yes," he somewhat agreed.

"Not met many who aren't. My count, all my life, that number equals two."

Those twinkling eyes stopped twinkling in order to flash.

"Just two?"

"Yup. Two," I confirmed.

"Although I find that knowledge upsetting, I'll share I'd like to make that three," he told me something I already (mostly) got.

"Listen, Marcus, this," I gestured between us with my hand and this time he didn't watch it, he didn't tear his gaze from my own "it's sweet, honey. Real sweet. Thanks for it. For the daisies. All that's real nice. But a woman lives the life I've lived and finds herself raped in a parking lot, she makes certain decisions. And those decisions don't include dinner with a hot guy who wears a suit real well, has a superior set of lips, and opens the door for her. She goes about her business her own damned self and that's that. I got me a good job. I got me a Porsche. I'm in the market to find me a house I like where I can garden and set the table like a good Southern woman should. What I don't got and don't *want* is a man."

"Would you allow me to try to change your mind about that?"

I shook my head and his eyes moved then, watching my hair shake with it.

They came back to mine when I answered, "Nope."

"Would you allow me to not allow you to not let me attempt to change your mind about that?"

That was convoluted for certain, but I still got him.

And what else I got was that I could probably repeat my "nope," but I knew he was going to find a way to try anyway.

He was just not going to succeed.

So I shrugged again and said, "Knock yourself out, darlin'."

His lips curled up again and I wished they hadn't because a normal curl was *fine*. A smile rocked my world.

The way they were right then set my coochie to tingling.

Seriously.

And my coochie hadn't tingled for *months*, not to mention no way *in hell* I thought it ever would again after my time on the asphalt out back.

"Dinner tomorrow," he said.

"No," I replied.

Slowly, his head tilted to the side and that hit my coochie too.

Damn.

"Thank you for speaking with me, Daisy."

He was ending this.

But he was absolutely not ending this.

Crap.

"Not a problem."

"Would you like me to escort you to your car or back to your friend?" he asked.

"Been gettin' around mostly okay on my own, honey bunch. So thanks. I'm good."

"Would you…like me to escort you to your car…or back to your friend?" he repeated, his words firmer, he took his time saying them and I got his message.

"I see this is gonna be interesting," I muttered.

"Agreed," he did not mutter.

We stared at each other.

This went on awhile.

Marcus ended it.

"You shouldn't have laughed."

"Pardon?"

"I might have let you be, but you laughed."

Oh Lord.

I didn't feel *that* in my coochie.

But I felt it.

Oh yeah, I felt it.

"Marcus—"

He cut me off. "To your friend. But I'll leave a man, and when you're ready, he'll be outside the dressing room and he'll escort you to your car."

"That isn't necessary."

"I know you think that. But you're wrong."

We did more staring until I sighed and mumbled, "Right."

I moved to the door.

He opened it for me.

He followed me down the stairs and at the bottom he put his hand again to my back as he escorted me to Chardonnay.

When we got to the dressing room, Ashlynn was there, too.

He left me there with only a murmured, "Ladies."

But he gave me a look that was a promise.

Hell.

He closed the door behind him.

"Okay, he totally scares me but I'd be on my back in about *a second* and my dreams of med school that I've had since I was twelve I'd totally blow off if that guy wanted to make me his moll, and I don't give one crap what that says about me," Chardonnay breathed the second the door latched.

"He just plain scares me," Ashlynn said, staring at me.

I ignored her and looked to Chardonnay.

"Girl, go rinse out that G-string and give it to me. I gotta get home. I got some glue gunning to do."

Chardonnay shook herself out of it, grinned at me, waggled her eyebrows, and then sashayed to the bathroom.

I took in a deep breath.

And then I let it go.

And I let it go sliding Marcus Sloan's card in the back pocket of my jeans.

Chapter Four

Steel Magnolias
Daisy

"These are fine. These are fine times about seven thousand. I *need* these."

"You've got seven thousand pairs of shoes, Tod. You don't *need* anything."

"Stevie, love of my life, are you not seeing these?"

"I'm seeing them."

"Then have you gone temporarily insane?"

"I'm thinking he has," a girl said.

"I'm thinking if he doesn't let you buy them, I'll get them and you can borrow them from me," another girl said.

"Sold!" the first (obviously gay) guy cried.

"Let's go," the first girl said. "Las Delicias has been there for years but I'm not taking any chances seeing as I need a beef burrito, STAT."

"Box 'em up and let's move, I'm hungry too," the second (also gay, seeing as he was the love of the other one's life) guy stated.

I sat with my back to them in chairs in the Nordstrom shoe department, listening to them go, and I didn't turn around to look at them. Not because I didn't want them to see my face. The bruises were fading good now so my conceal job was kickass.

But I did sit there thinking I needed a gay posse.

Especially if they went shoe shopping with you.

I also needed a girl posse.

But even though all the strippers were real nice, that wasn't my thing. I'd never managed to pull one of those together, even in the days when I'd put the effort in to try.

And since I didn't, I quit trying.

In my line of work, especially at Smithie's where he took care of the girls in a way they didn't feel the need to be catty, I might have been able to manage it.

The thing was, I was the headliner. The red velvet rope out front was for me.

I suspected Britney Spears was probably friendly with her dancers.

But they didn't go shoe shopping together.

And I didn't want to turn around in Nordstrom of all places (where some dreams came true, even if they did this to the tune of a credit card machine) to see what I was missing.

Not just then, but my entire life.

I knew I wasn't meant to have any kind of posse, as much as I'd always wanted it, and especially as much as it'd be good to have it right then after what had happened to me.

I just didn't need it staring me in the face when I didn't have it.

Instead, I looked down at the shoes I was trying on.

They cost twelve hundred dollars. They were class on a lollipop stick. Considering the serious hike in pay Smithie gave me a month ago, I could totally afford them (and could do that even before he jacked up my pay, but did it weirdly making me work less, but I didn't quibble).

And they were *so* not me.

"What do you think?" the shoe saleslady said.

"You got anything in denim?" I asked.

"Uh…no," she answered.

"Clear plastic, maybe with a daisy embedded in the platform?"

"Um…I don't think so."

"Slides with a seven-inch heel, three-inch platform, the whole thing bejeweled, maybe in pink?"

"Well…um, I think that's a no too, ma'am. I'm sorry."

I nodded.

I'd already learned Nordstrom shoe department didn't do Daisy.

It still didn't hurt to try.

I unbuckled the strappy sandal I had on and slid it off, murmuring, "That's okay. But thanks."

"Valentino does 'Rockstud,'" she informed me.

I'd checked out the Rockstud.

It wasn't all that bad.

But it didn't say *Daisy*.

"Not my thing," I shared, putting the sandal in the box, grabbing it, and handing it to her.

"Okay, well, if there's anything else you see you'd like to try, I'm here."

"Thanks, honey bunch, you're sweet."

I smiled at her.

She smiled at me and wandered away with the box.

I put on my shoes (black patent, platform sandal, one-inch rhinestone ankle strap, tube of rolled open red lipstick for a heel), got up, hitched up my purse on my shoulder, and glided to the makeup counter to while away more of my Saturday afternoon.

The shoe department might let me down in a variety of places.

But any makeup counter from Walgreens to Neiman's worked for me.

And that afternoon, it *so* did.

* * * *

The doorbell rang right in the middle of Julia Roberts having a diabetic fit in a salon chair in Dolly Parton's garage.

This did not make me happy.

Not Julia having a fit, of course, that never made me happy.

But I was right then not happy about my doorbell ringing during the best movie of all time.

I paused the movie, got up on my bare feet, and marched to the door in my hot-pink Juicy Couture tracksuit with the rhinestone, interlaced "JC" on the back with the crown on top surrounded with an oval of sparkles.

I looked through the peephole and I knew what I'd see because he'd told me he wasn't going to give up.

But he was interrupting *Steel Magnolias*.

No one did that.

Not even a tall, dark, rich, hot guy gentleman who opened doors for me.

And right then, even if he was not in a suit but looked just as f-i-n-e, *fine* in a V-necked, dark-blue sweater that did things to his eyes that, if I wasn't ticked about *Steel Magnolias*, would have done things to my coochie, and dark-wash jeans, he had to know that.

So I unlocked the deadbolt, slapped open the latch, and yanked open my own damned door.

"You're interrupting *Steel Magnolias*," I snapped tetchily to Marcus Sloan.

He burst out laughing.

He really shouldn't have done that.

He really shouldn't have laughed.

Really.

He was handsome, for sure, just as he was.

But laughter took years off his face.

Years.

I didn't know how old he was. He looked in his mid-thirties (and I wasn't going there seeing as he clearly had established his place in Denver at a young age which said something about him and what it said, to a girl like me, was *all* good).

But right then, he looked like the boy you hoped would neck with you (and you'd let him get to second base) after he took you to a movie.

Though, it was more.

The deep sumptuousness of his laughter felt like everything.

Every diamond in the world laid at your feet.

Every fur piled deep.

Every gold necklace a tangle of beauty twenty feet deep.

Still chuckling, he turned to the side and jerked his head toward my apartment, "Set it up."

Without a choice, I shifted out of the way as a tall, blond man wearing a black suit, white shirt, and thin black tie walked in carrying a paper bag by the handles in one hand and balancing a baker's box in the other.

Following him came a heavyset man dressed the exact same way.

He'd lost most of his steel gray hair and was for some reason wearing sunglasses even though the sun had gone down, not to mention, he was indoors. He had two bottles of champagne pressed to his chest in one arm, two delicate champagne flutes dangling from the other with...

I narrowed my eyes at them...

Beautiful peacocks engraved in the glass.

Really beautiful peacocks.

Perfection.

Damn him to hell.

I turned my narrowed eyes to Marcus as he moved in, putting a hand to my waist, and this time he used it to guide me where he wanted me to go.

Right smack dab into the middle of my living-slash-dining room.

I let this happen mostly because I was beginning to smell something.

Something so good it forced all of your attention to it.

Which meant I saw the first guy opening lids on food containers, the aroma of what was inside beating back the scent of flowers and filling the room.

"Barolo Grill," Marcus said and my suddenly food-dazed gaze drifted to him. "Prosciutto and melon. Lobster salad. Truffle risotto. And *bombolonis* for dessert. With Dom, of course."

With Dom, of course.

Dom Pérignon and lobster salad in my two-bedroom, not-much-to-write-home-about, uninspired-floorplan-like-gazillions-of-complexes-all-over-*the*-you-nited-States-of-America, galley kitchen, living-slash-dining-room, only-thing-good-about-it-was-the-master-bath apartment that I'd rented before I started to make a mint off stripping.

"Are you loco?" I asked.

His lips curled up. "No, I'm hungry." He turned his attention to his men. "That's good and that's all."

They started to move out but stopped when Marcus told them to do it.

His hand slid to the small of my back. "Daisy, this is my man, Brady, and my driver, Ronald."

In turn, first the blond, then the sunglassed man nodded to me.

"Pleased to meet you," Brady said.

"Same," Ronald grunted.

With nothing more, they both took off.

I watched the door close behind them and looked back at Marcus.

"You have a driver?"

"Yes."

"Why?"

"So he can drive me where I need to go."

I felt my eyes get squinty again.

He put pressure on my back and guided me to my not-much-to-write-home-about round dinette (that was *so* going to go when I got my fabulous new pad—there, I'd have a proper, Southern woman's dining room table, meaning big, gleaming, and covered in fine china, even if I didn't have any friends to sit at it) where they'd laid out the opened food cartons, baker's box, champagne, and flutes.

"I have a variety of concerns," he explained as we went. "Time is always in short supply. I can't use it wisely if I have to concentrate on driving. While Ronald drives, I can do things I couldn't if I was."

He stopped us by the table and I asked, "And you have a man?"

"I have several," he answered.

I gestured to the door with my hand. "So what's that one for?"

"Extra eyes."

"Extra eyes for what?"

He held my gaze steady. "For being certain, should someone think to do something stupid that I wouldn't very much like, they won't do that because they either saw Brady and got smart or Brady saw them and stopped them."

"So with these *concerns* of yours, you're constantly in danger," I guessed.

"No. Not many would be foolish enough to attempt to put me in a dangerous situation. What I am is cautious."

I nodded. "You sure strike fear in the hearts of the strippers, sugar. The ones who don't want to sleep with you, that is. But just sayin', they might wanna get laid by you, but you scare them too."

He grinned at me. "No offense, honey, but I'm not sure I consider strippers a threat."

"None taken, darlin', but gotta know. Do you consider anyone a threat?"

"No."

I tilted my head. "Is that smart?"

"I didn't work to earn my reputation by being stupid."

Hmm.

"You tryin' to scare me?" I asked.

"Absolutely not."

I held my breath at his tone and let him hold my gaze.

He did this until he wasn't feeling it anymore and he shared that by asking quietly, "Do you have plates?"

"I do. What I don't got is the desire to eat fancy shit in my house when I'm in the middle of the best movie of all time."

"We can eat in front of the television."

I offered an alternate scenario. "You can also call your boys, get your stuff, and mosey on down the road."

"I'm quite certain you know that's not going to happen."

I stared at him.

Then I sighed.

After that, I got plates.

I had fancy shit piled on one and a flute of champagne Marcus poured me in my hand while aiming my ass at my couch when I declared, "I'm not startin' it up again. I'm good to re-watch certain parts after it's done, like when Clairee is in that locker room. But I'm in the groove, even if it was interrupted, and I'm not re-startin' my groove."

"I'll catch up," Marcus told me, settling himself in my armchair, which was the only thing in my place I liked.

Supple leather. Big brass buttons studded all up the front and curve of the arms.

I bought it even though it didn't match my inexpensive twill couch and it cost a whack when I wasn't making a whack. I was schlepping drinks and wings at Hooters and wasn't doing too badly because my hooters put the "Hoot" in Hooters, but it didn't touch what I made stripping.

And I bought it because it looked like it belonged in a castle.

I wasn't looking at my chair.

I was looking at him.

"Pardon?"

He set his champagne on my side table.

"I'll catch up," he told me.

"What do you mean, you'll *catch up?*"

"How far into it are you?" he asked.

"I haven't gotten to the wedding yet."

His eyes twinkled.

Lord.

"I don't know what that means, honey," he said quietly.

"It means, not far."

"Then I'll catch up."

"You sayin' you haven't seen *Steel Magnolias?*"

He studied me even as he replied, "That's what I'm saying."

"How are you breathing on this earth, American, and haven't seen *Steel Magnolias?*"

His eyes kept twinkling.

Lord.

"I'm not certain how to answer that."

"It's the best movie of all time," I repeated my earlier declaration.

"We'll see."

We'll see?

"You don't get me, honey bunches of oats," I began. "It. Is. *The.* Best. *Movieofalltime.*"

He smiled at me. It was warm. Lush. Intimate. A thing of pure beauty.

I ignored that smile hitting my coochie.

"Play the movie, Daisy," he ordered.

"Don't tell me what to do," I snapped.

"Darling, please start the movie."

Crap.

That I felt in my coochie.

I glared at him, put down my champagne, snatched up the remote, and started the movie.

Needless to say, the food was great.

Also needless to say, the champagne was *fabulous.*

More needless to say, it didn't suck that Marcus not only didn't make me get up to get my *bombolonis*, he also didn't make me get up to fill my champagne flute.

And lastly, needless to say, when M'Lynn lost her nut by Shelby's casket and I lost my nut right along with her on my couch in my apartment no matter that I'd seen that scene one hundred and fifty times, I lost it again, a different way that time, when Marcus got up, nabbed my remote, and hit pause.

"*What are you doing?*" I screeched.

"We should not be watching this film."

Uh-oh.

I looked at his face.

He was looking at the tears on mine and he was not a happy man.

"Do you have a comedy?" he asked.

"This *is* a comedy," I informed him.

"You're crying."

"That's Southern for comedy," I educated.

"We just watched a young woman with a young child die, her mother standing there watching as she passed after her daughter was taken off life support. That is *not* a comedy, honey."

At that, for some *stupid* reason, I let loose.

"She got married to the man she loved. She gave him a baby. She had a momma who loved her. A daddy who adored her. Brothers who annoyed her but also adored her. Friends who thought the world of her. Her hubby was a lawyer who gave her a big house where she could make spaghetti in a big kitchen, even if she did pass out and slip into a diabetic coma in that kitchen. She had it all. She didn't have it for long but she at least had it. And she appreciated having it. She knew what it meant. And she knew how precious it was. And she left this world with that preciousness held deep in her heart. So she's good to wait with God until their time comes to join her because she entered those pearly gates knowin' she left the world having everything she needed."

Marcus stood by me sitting on the couch, staring down at me, and I felt his look like he wasn't standing removed and staring at me, but like he was close, holding me in his arms like he loved me, only me, had forever, and would forever and always.

"That might not say comedy," I pushed out in a whisper, trying to get past his look. "But Ouiser and Clairee are about to rip the lid off, sugar. You just haven't gotten to that part yet."

"Do you have a momma who loves you?" he asked abruptly.

I pressed my lips together.

He watched.

Then he bit out, "Right." His gaze went from my lips to my eyes. "A daddy?"

"Marcus—"

Just at me saying his name, he got me.

That's why he interrupted me and went on.

"Brothers?"

I shook my head.

"Sisters?"

I bit my lip.

"Right," he repeated softly.

"Can we watch the movie?" I whispered.

In response, immediately, he sat next to me. He also stretched out his legs, crossed his ankles, and put his arm around me, pulling me into his side.

As I was curled into the corner of the sofa, my legs under me, my plate gone, my champagne in my hand, I wasn't able to do anything but teeter more fully into him so he had all my weight.

I tried to pull away.

I stopped when he announced, "You move, Daisy, this once, right now, watching this fucking movie, I won't let you."

Well, that was clear enough.

"Roger that," I muttered.

"Settle," he growled.

Oh boy.

I felt that in my coochie too.

I pressed my lips together again and did as told.

"Fuck," he went back to muttering, lifted the remote, and started the movie again.

As I told him, within minutes, Ouiser and Clairee ripped the lid off.

Even so, Marcus didn't let me go.

He kept hold of me.

And he didn't stop.

Not for the whole rest of the movie.

* * * *

We stood in my open doorway.

Marcus was leaving.

I was marveling at the fact that at his texted command, Marcus's men showed, cleared everything, even to the point of cleaning the flutes and putting the plates in the dishwasher (but even if they cleared everything, they put the extra bottle of Dom in the fridge and left the flutes). Then they took off leaving Marcus and me at the door.

I was also marveling at the fact that Marcus didn't mind that I rewound to the locker room scene (and played it twice).

Since my mind was otherwise occupied, it came as a surprise when his hand fell light as it cupped my cheek.

My body jerked and my eyes darted up to his.

"Please don't touch me."

His hand dropped away but this time he didn't move away.

He shifted closer. In my space. Not threatening. Not pushy. Just...*there*.

"Have you talked to someone?" he asked gently.

"I'm talkin' to you now," I pointed out.

"About what happened to you, honey."

I looked to the side.

"Please, darling, look at me."

I pressed my lips together, drew in breath through my nose, and looked up at him again.

"You need to talk to somebody," he urged.

"I'm doin' a-okay," I shared.

"You have trouble with me touching you."

"You find that surprising?" I asked a little sarcastically.

"No. My fear is that, if you don't speak to someone about it, you won't be able to get past it."

I shook my head. "Had a lot of shit happen to me in my life, sugar. This is just another load a' shit I gotta get around. And make no mistake, like all the others, I'll get around this."

His brows went up. "And it's necessary for you to do it on your own?"

"All a girl's got is herself."

That's when Marcus Sloan rocked my world.

He did this by declaring, "You're entirely wrong."

"I—" I began and I got that one letter out but it didn't count because he talked right over me saying it.

"A woman like you should have had a momma who loved her. A daddy who adored her. Friends who thought the world of her. She should have grown up every day knowing that straight to her soul, never doubting it, not for a second."

I felt my eyes narrow for no other reason than to beat back what his words were making me feel.

"You don't know what kind of girl I am."

"I know precisely the kind of woman you are, Daisy. And if *you* don't understand it, then it'll be up to me to show it to you."

Oh Lord.

Time to try another tack.

"Marcus, I'm tellin' you, you don't got a pla—"

He put his hand up between us and shook his head, cutting me off saying an impatient, "No."

I kept trying.

"The food was real good and it was sweet, you bein' all..." I didn't know how to express the gorgeousness of it so I used the universal, "whatever with me when M'Lynn lost it at Shelby's funeral. And I'm not sayin' I haven't hit a rough patch. I know I have. I'm not in denial or nothin'. I'm workin' through it, but doin' that *my way*. What I'm sayin' is, this is sweet and all, but you don't have a place in that."

"You've made that clear. I just don't agree."

Again, I was getting mad.

"Okay then, I'll explain it this way. I'm not gettin' used to some fine man showin' me attention, bringin' me fancy food and bein' sweet only to hit that time when I get my gold bracelet and a good-bye."

He stared down at me, something flitting through his eyes.

Then he murmured, "Ah."

"Ah, what?" I snapped.

It was then he got closer. Still not threatening, but coming on strong.

I held my breath.

"It's understandable, in a sense, that you'd say that. You don't know me. But I'll tell you and then I'll *show* you that I am not a man who would come into a woman's life, a woman who had what happened to you happen to her, with the intention of doing what I had to do to get what I wanted and then give her my good-bye." He drew in breath and didn't release my gaze when he finished, "Although understandable, it's still insulting as all fuck."

I blinked and felt my stomach twist painfully.

He shifted back.

"Goodnight, Daisy."

And with that, he turned, walked down the hall, and disappeared.

Chapter Five

Prince Charming
Daisy

I woke up in a cold sweat.

And terrified.

I didn't even think. I couldn't coordinate my limbs. So when I moved, I fell off my bed, right to the floor. I crawled half the distance to the door to my bedroom before I found my feet.

Once I did, I sprinted to the dinette where I'd left my purse. I snatched out my cell and sprinted back to my room, slamming the door, locking the lock, so lost in my head, when I ran across the room, I thumped into my bed, falling on top of it, but I didn't hesitate.

I scrambled over it and off the other side, hitting the floor on my hands. The cell digging into my palm, I just kept going. My knees falling off the bed, crashing into the floor, I crawled to the corner, turned, pressed my back in, lifted my knees up protectively in front of me, and fumbled my phone as I brought it to my face.

I flipped it open and saw it tremble in my hand as I searched for the number I'd programmed in no matter I knew it was a fool thing to do.

I was glad I'd done it then.

I hit it, put the phone to my ear, and felt it shaking against the shell.

I heard it ring.

It rang four times, and with each passing one I wanted to scream before I heard a deep man's voice say, "Yes?"

"M-M-Marcus, I do-don't...I just had a..." I gulped, "I c-c-can't—"

"Daisy," he stated urgently, "is someone there?"

"I, no, I...y-y-es...um, no."

I was making no sense and didn't even know it. I was too busy realizing that my teeth were chattering, and worse, I couldn't do a thing about it.

I sensed vaguely he sounded like he was on the move as he asked, "Where are you?"

"B-b-bedroom."

"Stay there. In a few minutes, the man I have on your apartment will be in your apartment. His name is Louie. He'll call out his name so you'll know he's there. He won't approach. I'll be there as soon as I can."

"O-o-kay."

"As soon as I can, darling. Yes?"

"Y-yeah."

"I have to let you go now."

"Yeah."

"Be right there," he whispered.

"Yeah," I repeated, unable to say anything else, trembling so badly I was quaking.

I heard the disconnect like it was far away instead of right at my ear but I didn't take the phone away. I held it there until my hand floated down, the phone still flipped open, and I stared through the dark at the door.

"It's Louie!" I heard yelled from my living room and I jumped, crying out quietly, tucking my knees tight to my chest, wrapping my arms around them. "All clear!" he shouted. "All good! Mr. Sloan is on his way."

I didn't say thank you. I didn't say anything.

I didn't think anything either.

I didn't think how I'd been a bitch to Marcus after he'd been nothing but kind and patient with me. Sending me daisies. Bringing me Dom. Being gentle and sweet.

It had been a week since that night and I'd heard nothing from him. Saw nothing of him.

But the daisies kept coming.

As they did, I thought it was that he forgot he was sending them, and the minute the bill showed, he'd cancel them.

I didn't allow myself to think further on that.

For a number of reasons, I'd wanted to call. To apologize.

It was what a good Southern woman should do, for one.

But it was what *I* wanted to do. Me. Daisy. For him. Marcus. To make it better. To take it back. To let him know that I wanted to be like Shelby from *Steel Magnolias*. Strong like her. Strong enough to know that it was better to have a little bit of something wonderful than a lifetime of just plain nothing.

Then explain to him that he had to go because I couldn't allow myself to have a little bit of something wonderful knowing it'd be taken away.

I was just not that strong.

It wasn't just about a man like Stretch knowing he shouldn't leave me with my mother, and doing it anyway. Maybe because he had no claim to me. But mostly, I reckoned, because he wasn't strong enough either.

And it wasn't just about Miss Annamae giving me all I needed to live my life right, but not being around long enough for me to show her I'd listened to every word.

It was about being the kind of girl that the only good thing a man had given her was a really fantastic boob job and no matter how much she fought and scratched and worked for a little hint of peace in her life, she still got herself raped on the blacktop of a parking lot.

So I didn't call Marcus. I didn't apologize. I didn't explain. I thought it best to leave him be.

I didn't care what he did for a living. He deserved better.

Much, much better than me.

The bruising was gone, most of the scrapes had healed, and I was going to go back to the stage next Saturday.

I'd wanted to do it that night but Smithie was not big on that idea. He wanted me to take more time. He wanted me to talk to some woman LaTeesha had found, a woman named Bex, who worked at some rape crisis center. And then he wanted me to give it a month or two, still paid leave, and he also wanted me to move in with him and LaTeesha for a spell.

I'd put my foot down. We'd had words.

After sharing I was a pain in his ass, he'd given in but only if I'd give it another week.

I could do that so I'd agreed.

But I didn't think of any of that. Not right then, cowering on my ass in the corner of my darkened bedroom, some man I didn't know in my living room who another man I'd insulted had watching my apartment to keep me safe.

I just stared through the dark at the door, doing it like the fool I was, the coward, quaking on my ass in the dark.

I heard the knob on the door jostle and then Marcus calling, "Stay where you are, honey."

That wasn't hard since I couldn't move.

There was some muted scraping before light poured in from the living room as the door opened and I winced at the bright.

Almost before it illuminated the room, it was gone, and I stared as Marcus's tall shadow moved toward me.

I thought he'd stop, and with him there, his man outside, I tried to pull myself together. The humiliation of cringing in a corner beginning to dawn, the feel of it spreading over me.

He didn't stop.

He made it to me, bent low, gathered me up and then he went right back down. Situating himself exactly as I had been in the corner but without the trembling and with me in his lap, held close to his chest, one arm tight around me, the other one slanted up my back, fingers in my hair, pressing my face to his throat.

I felt his strength. His warmth. Smelled hints of his cologne.

"What happened?" he whispered. "Nightmare?"

At that word, it came rushing in, and I wasn't strong enough to beat it back.

And because I wasn't, I couldn't help myself. I didn't even feel myself do it.

But I did it.

I burrowed into him, grasping his sweater in my fists, shoving into him like I wanted his flesh to soak me in and take away the fear, the shame, a life that was mostly misery.

"Okay, okay," he soothed, his hold on me tightening. "Shh. I'm right here. Right here, honey."

"I got...I gotta build my castle," I told him mindlessly.

"I'm sorry?"

"But I can't. I can't build no more castles. I don't got it in me."

I was unconsciously rocking.

"Castles?"

I shoved my face in his throat and kept rocking.

"A moat. Big studded door no one can break through. Stone three feet thick. Keepin' me safe. Keepin' me safe." I sounded like I was chanting but it didn't matter. I wasn't even aware of what I was saying. "I build my castles so they can keep me safe." I swallowed, hard. It hurt and it felt like Marcus felt it too because his arms got even tighter and he took over rocking me. "Just in my mind. They were always just in my mind. So they couldn't keep me safe."

"You're safe now."

"I've never been safe."

He shifted, his arms folding me into myself so I was a little ball of Daisy held closely against him, "Okay, darling, but you're safe now."

"I wanna believe that. I wanna believe in castles."

"You'll believe," he whispered.

"I wanna believe."

"You'll believe, Daisy."

I said nothing. His warmth and scent and arms around me, rocking me gently with his body, started penetrating and I pushed in deeper.

The trembling was easing, my mind blanking, my eyelids heavy when I heard Marcus ask, "In your castle, did you have a prince charming?"

And as I gave up the fight, allowed my eyes to close, I muttered, "There ain't no prince charming for a girl like me."

With that, I drifted to sleep.

* * * *

My eyes opened and I saw daisies.

But I smelled bacon.

I dropped to my back in bed and stared at the ceiling, the night before washing over me.

"Shit," I mumbled.

I turned again, to my belly, snatching up my other pillow and shoving my face in it.

I smelled Marcus's cologne.

"Shit," I repeated but it was muffled to come out sounding like, "Shfft."

I pushed the pillow away, rolled again, tossing back the covers and pulling myself out of bed.

I wandered to my bathroom, flipped on the light, and went to the mirror.

I looked into it.

Well, at least that was good.

As any good Southern woman should, I had a big head of hair. And like every girl who knew good hair knew, you didn't wash it every day and with every day you didn't wash it, the natural product God gave you made it look better and better.

I was on day three. My hair looked full, the curls I'd set in it with my hot rollers were still bouncy but now a bit flippy, and it was cute. Not to mention, one of the only good things my momma gave me, radiant skin, looked just that (even if I had a nuance of dark circles under my eyes).

I opened a drawer and grabbed some hair ties. Using them, I tamed my curls into pigtails. Then I went about my routine: brush teeth, floss, cleanser with exfoliation, brush out of lashes, and smoothing of brows.

And even though I only had on a pair of silk pajamas (shorts with a deep, *deep* edge of hollow-out lace and a camisole of the same but a shorter edge of lace at the top and cute little cream bows at each hip, the rest of it all in the shade of pistachio), I walked out of my bathroom and right to my kitchen.

Marcus was at my stove. He was wearing another V-necked sweater, this one light blue, and another pair of jeans that weren't dark-wash but they weren't faded either.

His feet were bare. His hair was slightly tousled. And I wanted to say after the mortification of my drama last night that the sight of him at a skillet in my kitchen looking like that I didn't feel in my coochie.

But that was a lie.

I totally felt the sight of him looking like that in my kitchen in my coochie.

His eyes came to me.

Oh yeah.

Right in the coochie.

I'd opened my mouth to say something, but at the look on his face, any words got trapped in my throat and I quit breathing entirely.

"Come here," he ordered gently.

My feet took me right there.

Still with a fork in his hand, his other arm wrapped around me and he pulled me close so my front was pressed to his side, his chin dipping into his neck to keep his gaze on me.

"Okay?" he whispered.

I nodded.

"Hungry?" he asked.

I nodded again.

"Good," he murmured, giving me a squeeze and turning his attention to the bacon.

He was shifting it around in the skillet and I was watching him do this in a weird haze.

But the haze, as hazes are wont to do, even ones you had standing in your kitchen pressed close to a hot guy, cleared.

I tipped my head back and started, "Marcus—"

The instant his name passed my lips, he again dipped his chin into his neck and I clamped my mouth shut at the new look in his eyes.

"I have a man looking for him. I've hired a private investigator to look for him. And two of my colleagues are looking for him. When one of them finds him, they will not take him to the police. They'll bring him to me. And I'll be dealing with him personally."

Oh.

My.

"How're you gonna do that?" I asked softly.

"I'm going to put a bullet in his forehead."

Oh my!

I stared up at him.

"In the meantime," he went on like he didn't just tell me he planned to assassinate my rapist, "although I figure you know this now, you are not unsafe. You're watched twenty-four-seven. I have a man on you at all times. When you're trying on shoes. When you're grocery shopping. When you're up in this apartment watching movies. No one you don't want near you will get near you."

After delivering that, he looked to the bacon and flipped it.

I watched him do this wordlessly.

When he was done, I felt his gaze come back to me and I gave him mine.

"Is that understood?" he asked.

"Uh...yeah."

"Right. Excellent. Next topic. I want you to move into my condo with me."

Uh-oh.

"Uh...no."

"Daisy—"

"Honey, you're bein' all kinds of sweet. You've *been* all kinds of sweet. Even after I was a bitch to you and you didn't deserve it."

"You're going through a good deal."

"You still didn't deserve it."

He inclined his head, conceding the point like only a gentleman would.

Lord.

"And I appreciate it," I continued. "Last night wasn't good. But it happened and now I can get a lock on it. I promise. *Swear*. It means a lot to me you stepped up when I called. I feel bad I did that, pullin' you from your bed in the middle of the night, but it felt good you stepped up and did it so sweet. But I'll get a lock on it. That's a certainty. So I'm good now and I'm not movin' in with you."

"Then I'll move in with you."

"Marcus—"

He slid the bacon off the burner, switched it off, set the fork aside, and then turned fully into me, wrapping his other arm around me.

"Last night wasn't not good, Daisy. Last night was *bad*. The time it took for me to get to you, I could tell with one look at you in that corner, you were in hell. After I got to you, it didn't get much better. I'm not allowing that to happen again."

"But, now it's happened, I can—"

"I have a guest room. It's nice. You can stay in there. Alternately, if you prefer to be in your own home, since you don't have a guest room set up, I'll sleep on your couch if that's where you wish me to be."

"This is—"

"And you need to talk to someone about what happened to you."

I felt my eyes get squinty. "Will you let me finish?"

"Not if you say things that, I'm sorry, darling, aren't smart. You're not looking after yourself. You're not letting Smithie and LaTeesha look after you. And since you're not, I'm stepping in."

"You been gone a week," I pointed out snappily.

"You needed time, and I assessed from our last conversation, space. I gave it to you. You curled up, terrified in a corner, I'm done doing that."

"You don't get it."

"No, I don't. You've attempted to explain and I still don't. Mostly because I never got the concept of bullshit and I still don't, even when a beautiful woman is trying to feed it to me."

Honestly?

I couldn't take any more.

And because I couldn't, something snapped in me.

It snapped inside and it snapped me right out of his arms.

I took a step back but lifted my hands and planted them in his chest, shoving him.

He rocked back on a foot but I retreated three, lifted my hand, and jabbed a finger at him.

"*You don't get it!*" I shrieked.

"Then give it to me," he whispered.

The change in his tone didn't register on me. The look on his face.

Nothing.

"I forgot my lip gloss. *My lip gloss!*" I screamed. "Not my tips. Not my phone. Not somethin' important. My…fucking…*lip gloss.*"

"Okay, honey," he said gently.

"Went back for fucking *lip gloss*."

"All right, Daisy."

"Out of the blue," I swung my raised arm wide and dropped it, "he jumps me. Do you know how it feels to be somewhere you think you're safe, doin' something you got every right to do, and some asshole jumps you?"

"No."

"It doesn't feel real good," I shared.

Marcus didn't say anything.

"I can take a slap. I can take the back of a hand. Daddy taught me that. Not to mention a number of Momma's other men who had that kinda thing honed *real* good."

I watched his jaw get hard, a muscle shift up his cheek, but that didn't register on me either.

"I can even take a punch. More than one asshole I let in there gave me that lesson."

"Christ," he bit out.

I ignored that and the emotion behind it.

"But that, *that*, and what he gave me after he gave me my beating, *that* I hadn't been taught."

"No woman needs that lesson."

"Well, I got it," I snapped.

"And he'll get his."

"Right, with you puttin' a bullet in his brain?"

"Precisely."

I cocked my head to the side, feeling my hair move with me, and ground out, "You barely know me and you got that much feelin' for me you're willin' to take that on your soul?"

"Yes."

At that, the firmness of it, the simplicity, *I* rocked back like *he'd* shoved *me*.

"You don't want me to do that, he didn't rape me. That's your call," he stated. "I'll have him brought to the police. You don't give a fuck about that asshole, he's dead. At my hand. And I won't take pleasure from it. But it cannot be denied, when it's done, it won't give me satisfaction."

"Now you *are* tryin' to scare me," I accused.

"No." He shook his head. "In my world, actions have consequences. You are far from dumb, Daisy. You know the world I live in. You might not know the rules but you know there are rules. And no one breaks them. If they do, they suffer retribution as decreed by the laws of the street. He violated my turf and I mean that in the sense I own part of Smithie's. But he violated something that's just plain *mine* and for that, he suffers the ultimate reckoning."

Lord.

He was killing me.

"I'm not yours," I whispered.

"Honey, please start paying attention."

At that, I shut up.

Marcus didn't do the same.

"That's the man I am, Daisy," he declared. "And that's going to happen regardless of what I say next. Which is, right now, you have one chance. If what I just shared scares you. If it turns your stomach. If it's something that you don't want in your life, I'll walk away. You can have all the bacon and you'll never see me again. But if you don't say…right now…that's something you can't take, then we're sharing the bacon, the eggs I'm going to make, and a whole lot more when the time is right."

At the thought of never seeing him again, I wrapped my arms around my stomach and kept my eyes glued to him.

Marcus didn't move. He kept watching me. He did it silently.

And as he did it, something settled in him, in his frame and in his face.

It was a sight to see. A thing of beauty.

And it scared me spitless.

After a while, he spoke, his voice just as firm but a whole lot more gentle.

"In terms I hope you'll understand, darling, in fairytales, the prince vanquishes the wicked queen. The evil stepmother. The malicious goblin. In real life, Daisy, to avenge wrong done to his princess, if the need arises, the prince puts a bullet in somebody's brain."

Yes.

Killing me.

Without me telling it to do it, my mouth whispered, "Why?"

"I just explained why."

"No." I shook my head. "Why me?"

I asked and Marcus didn't hesitate even a second to answer.

"Because my mother left me when I was six. She wasn't a loss. She left me with my father, who was a decent enough father, a good man, but a stupid one and very weak. We didn't have much because he wasn't capable of giving me much, but there were more reasons. We didn't live in squalor. However, the little we had wasn't much better. Then, when I was ten, he'd gotten himself under the weight of a debt he couldn't repay since he made dick but he also liked to play the ponies. They busted out his knees first. Then they took his thumbs. After that, they took his life."

"Oh my God," I breathed.

"He had a daughter from another relationship, my half-sister. She grew up with her mother and she didn't have much either. The good in my dad, he made sure my sister was in my life. As much as we could be, we were close. When Dad was killed, she was all I had left. And she had a choice. Take me on or let me go into the system. She took me on. She was twenty. And she put a roof over my head, food on the table, and a lot of love in my life. But the first two things she gave me, she did it stripping."

Understanding dawned, I felt my body jolt and then I felt my face set.

Marcus didn't miss it.

"Stop right now thinking what you're thinking," he clipped out.

"Hard not to, sugar," I returned.

"She married a man twenty-five years older than her when I was sixteen. It was a love match. They haven't slept a single night without each other since their wedding and they retired to Florida five years ago. He was definitely a good guy and definitely decent. But he didn't have much either, though he did his best. They retired to a four-bedroom house with a pool that's in a development that has three top-notch golf courses because I worked my ass off to make certain that would be the way they ended their years together."

I ignored all this, no matter how hard that kind of beautiful generosity was to ignore, and I did it in order to ask cuttingly, "You savin' your sister in this fairytale of yours that you're corrallin' me into, Marcus?"

"No," he answered immediately.

But he wasn't done.

"I had a mother I barely remember, a trail of women my father couldn't keep, and a sister who loves me maybe more than the three kids she had with Doug because we toughed it out together. We had bad times. We had lean times. We had everyone around us treating us like shit because they thought they knew who we were by what she did and how my father was. We had interfering teachers telling themselves they were doing the honorable thing by trying to take me away from her. Most important in all that, we had a family. It was just the two of us but she loved me and I loved her and that was all we needed. She gave me a great deal. And right now, what you need to know that she gave me is the understanding of exactly the kind of woman I would eventually claim as mine."

"And what kind is that?"

"One who's beautiful. One who's smart. One who's kind. One who's strong. One who doesn't give a shit what people think about her. One who'd do what she could for anyone who asked no matter if it isn't convenient or easy. One who knows what having nothing feels like so she knows what matters and to appreciate it when she gets it."

"And you think that's me?"

"No. I know it's you."

"You're sure," I scoffed.

He looked around the kitchen and then back at me, lifting up his hands at his sides, and sounding exasperated when he asked, "What do you think I'm doing here?"

I knew what he was doing there.

Just, for his sake—primarily how much more awesome all that he was telling me made him—no matter how damned stubborn he was being about it, I knew he shouldn't be.

"I'm sorry you had to go through that in your life," I said with feeling. "I get it and I'm not thrilled to learn that we got a lot in common with the shit we actually got in common, sugar. But just to say, that woman is not me."

One second, he was four feet away.

The next second he was in my space, both hands cupping my cheeks, his eyes all I could see.

"I've been waiting thirty-five years for you to come into my life, Daisy," he whispered fiercely.

And again I stopped breathing.

But Marcus didn't stop talking.

"You can twist it into me wanting to save my sister from the life she had to lead to take care of me. Into me wanting a piece of your ass. Into whatever the fuck you want to try to twist it into. But since I was a kid, I knew what kind of life I intended to lead and that was to be so far away from the life I grew up in with my dad, I wouldn't even remember how that felt. And I knew I'd do whatever I had to do to get it, without doubts, without indecision, without remorse. And last, baby, I knew the woman I'd have by my side when I got there. So twist it whatever way you want. I'll find a way to untwist it because something else I know, when I find what I know without a doubt I want, without remorse, I'll find a way to get it."

I opened my mouth to speak but froze when his lips brushed mine and stayed there.

"Shut up," he said even though I didn't speak a word. "Bacon's laying in its grease and the eggs aren't going to make themselves. So pour yourself a goddamned cup of coffee and relax. We'll have breakfast and then we'll dance more of this dance later. Right now, I'm hungry."

Marcus was hungry.

Hearing that, the fight just left me and I whispered, "Okay."

"Okay," he whispered back, brushed his lips against mine again, staring into my eyes *this close*, his blue ones warm and sweet and twinkling.

Then he let me go and went back to the bacon.

* * * *

Marcus made me put a robe on before he took my hand and walked me to the door.

We stood in it like we'd done last Saturday night, except he was a lot closer.

Someone was in the mood to be pushy.

"We're having dinner tonight," he announced.

I rolled my eyes to the ceiling.

When I'd rolled them back, his hand was cupping my jaw and his face was even closer.

And his damned eyes were twinkling.

"You are beautiful," he declared out of the blue. "You're funny. You're challenging, and by that I mean stubborn, and even if it can be aggravating, I still like it. I *very* much like your choice of nightwear. I also like your legs, breasts, hair, and eyes. I'd commit murder to hear your laugh again, and I intend to, not a figure of speech, being real. Last but very much not least, I more than like the fact that when I gave you an out, you didn't take it, even if it's maddening you don't realize what you not taking it means. But even with all of that, darling, you are a serious pain in the ass."

Well!

"I didn't take that out because I didn't want you to think I was judgey," I retorted (and lied, but I wasn't going there even in my head).

"You didn't take that out because you like me," he fired back, shifting his hand so it slid to curl around the back of my neck as he curved his other arm around me. "You know every step of your life was leading you right here. You're the woman for me, which means, darling, I'm the man for you. And you didn't tell me to leave because you know that just the same as me."

"Now you're bein' cocky, which isn't real attractive, honey bunch."

Another lie, dammit.

He grinned. "More bullshit. More of a pain in my ass."

"You could leave," I suggested.

He didn't leave.

His hand at my neck moved up to cup my scalp, his head came down, and he kissed me.

Soft, sweet, the tip of his tongue traced the crease of my lips, and just when I was about to open them for him (the thought didn't even cross my mind to pull away, and I wasn't going there either), he lifted his head.

I opened eyes I hadn't even realized I'd closed.

"Now," he whispered, his grin even more cocky than he'd just been, his gaze roaming my face and doing it with satisfaction so I knew exactly what I was exposing, damn him all to hell, "I'll leave.

Dinner tonight, honey. I'll be here at seven."

"And I'll be in Timbuktu."

"Book into a five-star, darling. I'll meet you there and I'll pay."

Damn.

He had a comeback for everything!

I rolled my eyes again.

I heard him chuckle, felt his lips touch my nose then his hold leave me, and I watched him walk down the hall.

He stopped halfway and turned back to me.

Then he tore something from me. Something that had been fixed to me. Something I didn't ask for. Something I didn't deserve. Something I didn't want.

Something I didn't know how to get rid of that was so heavy, it was a miracle it hadn't crushed me.

And the only reason it hadn't crushed me was that I had help keeping it buoyed up with an apartment full of daisies.

He did that by stating, "If you think your lip gloss is important, it is. You were correct. You have every right in every way in everything to do what you wish to do, go where you wish to go, be what you wish to be. No one has the right to take that away. It isn't the lip gloss. It isn't the man at Smithie's who left his post. It's the fact an animal was loose that night. A monster. And he caught you in the dark. No one is to blame but him. No one should shoulder that but him. And no one will. But him."

I stood staring at Marcus, breathing heavily, having had to put my hand up and hold on to the edge of the door while his words sheared a burden the size of a mountain from me.

"Do you understand that, darling?" he asked.

I nodded.

"Good," he said. "Tonight, Daisy, seven. And if you need anything before then, you know how to contact me or just come down to my man watching your apartment and ask. I don't give a fuck you're about out of coffee. He'll send someone to get it for you."

Oh.

My.

Lord.

"Now do you understand that?" he pressed, and that question

was important. More important than it seemed. So important, my answer was going to change my life.

I knew it. I knew it better than I knew the best ways to rat my hair to give it maximum volume.

And in that moment, I had no choice in the answer I gave.

I nodded.

"Good," he whispered, his blue eyes warming me from six feet away to the point my toes curled in, I was just that toasty.

Then he was gone.

Chapter Six

Patch of Light
Daisy

"If you're feelin' the love for rock 'n' roll, tonight at Herman's Hideaway, hit up a new band that's made the scene, Stella and The Blue Moon Gypsies. The lead singer has been rockin' clubs in Denver for a while. But she's found her groove with the Gypsies. Trust me, I caught them as an opening act at the Gothic last weekend and they blew the roof off. To get you into the feel, I'll play a song Stella and her crew kill when they cover it. La Grange, by ZZ Top."

The radio was playing while I was getting ready for Marcus to take me out to dinner.

I was a Southern girl, which meant I was a country girl. I could kick back to the sound of Patsy, Loretta, Barbara, Tammy, Emmylou, Shania, Wynonna, Trisha, Reba, and the best of all time, Dolly.

But there were times in my life when I had to switch to something else with deep Southern roots.

That's when I hit up my rock 'n' roll.

And in my getup, it was a rock 'n' roll night sure as certain.

Obviously, I'd decided to go out with Marcus.

He wanted to convince me we were meant to be together, he'd been kind enough to me he'd earned that shot.

But he was going to know what he was getting.

To this end, I was wearing my leopard print (or one of them). A skintight mini-dress that only went down to *there*. The back was scooped all the way out and the front was scooped to maximum cleavage potential (and with the maximums of my cleavage, this might be awe-inspiring to some; heck, it was my cleavage and it was still that to me).

I was going to pair this with my sky-high platform sandals with the black patent across the balls of my feet, open toes to show off the new fire-engine-red pedicure I'd given myself (along with the same in a manicure, but on my long talons, I'd added a curve of amber rhinestones all along one side of the outer edge of each ring finger). The platform and heel of the shoes were covered in leopard.

My hair was even more sky-high than my platforms. Teased to mammoth proportions at the top and sides, I'd smoothed that back and then curled the hell out of the rest of my tresses so they fell in soft, defined swirls from a high-rise at the crown all the way down my back (the bangs were blown out straight and brushing my forehead).

My makeup was how I'd do it if I was stripping, which was how I'd do it when I wasn't stripping. My eyes weren't smoky. They were *smoke*. My skin bronzed. The sides of my nose and under my cheekbones shaded. My cheeks a dewy tangerine. My lips a nude-y, super-glossed, glittering peach.

I had in bronze chandelier earrings that nearly swept my shoulders and were liberally dosed with black and amber beads. A bronze statement necklace practically covered my upper chest and I had so many dangly bracelets on, if Marcus got through the night without the noise of them tinkling driving him to murder *me*, he'd definitely pass an important test.

I thought I looked *divine*. I had a cute little body, fantastic bosoms, a whole lot of thick hair, and skin to die for, and everything I'd done to augment it only made it that much better.

I also knew that not a lot of people agreed with me.

But Miss Annamae had told me to embrace my style when I found it (and boy had I found it) and not to let anyone cut me down.

Personally, I thought every woman should have at least one leopard print item in her closet. I didn't care if it was just a clutch and I also didn't care if that woman usually wore oxford shirts and loafers. She still needed leopard.

If someone didn't agree with me on that, or my platforms, my big hair, and my heavy hand with eyeliner, they could go fuck themselves.

This was my thought as I leaned over the basin, whisking on one last coat of lip gloss and listening to ZZ Top when I heard, "Daisy."

I jumped a mile, whirled, and cried, "*Lord!*"

I also saw Marcus lounging in the doorway to my bathroom.

"You scared the dickens out of me!" I snapped loudly, shoving the wand of the gloss back in the tube.

He sauntered in, reached out to my portable, and turned down the music.

He then leaned a hip against my bathroom counter like it was *his* bathroom counter, crossed his arms on his chest and stated, "I knocked. For five minutes. To ascertain if I needed to purchase a ticket to Timbuktu, I let myself in. Not easy for you to hear a knock over that music, honey."

"It isn't seven yet," I retorted.

"It's twelve past."

I didn't have a clock in the bathroom and I wasn't wearing a watch, and further, there was no reason for him to lie. So I just did the only option available to me.

I formed my mouth into a pout.

He grinned at me.

"If it's twelve past and you knocked for five minutes, either you're shit at pickin' a lock or you're late," I noted.

His grin became a smile I felt in my coochie.

God!

"Just something to know about me," he began, "I'm not shit at picking a lock."

"I'll file that away," I replied but didn't stop speaking. "Just something to know in order to just know it, it ain't polite to sneak up on a woman and it *really* ain't polite to interrupt her gettin' ready for your date."

His eyes did a sweep of me.

I felt *that* in my nipples (and my coochie).

"You're not ready?"

I was.

I just needed to put my shoes on.

"I don't have my shoes on."

"Not sure shoes can make all that better," he said low. "But I bet if anyone could manage that, it'd be you."

I tried to remain annoyed; I just couldn't.

"You've messed up the opportunity to see the full show," I pointed out.

"Trust me, darling, when I get it, it won't be unappreciated."

With his response, I finally took him in.

He was wearing a blue suit, a crisp light-blue shirt, and a silk tie in a blue that was three shades darker than the suit and had a matching pocket square. His dark hair was thick. The cut gave him fullness at the top without it looking overly styled, short but not buzzed at the sides and back, and unlike that morning, when it was messy and falling over his forehead, it was now swept back from his handsome face.

He looked *GQ*.

I looked like Dolly Parton impossibly created a love child with Peg Bundy (no, I *rocked* that look).

But suddenly, my stomach felt like it was sinking.

"Daisy?"

My focus returned to him.

He'd sensed the feeling I had.

How had he done that?

No. No. Marcus Sloan being scarily adept at tuning himself to me was something I was not going to think about. Not then. Not anytime soon. Maybe not ever.

"Daisy," he prompted gently.

"We don't match," I said quietly.

"I'm sorry?"

"You're *GQ*. I'm Peg Bundy."

He gave one nod, declaring, "Yes, and lose the cigarette, Peg Bundy was gorgeous."

I stared.

Then I asked, "Are you being serious with me?"

His brows drew together. "Are *you* being serious asking that question?"

I nodded my head and felt my hair go with it.

Marcus watched my hair. His lips quirked then he looked at me.

"She was supposed to be funny, she was in a sitcom," he

reminded me.

"Right," I whispered.

"That didn't make her any less beautiful."

"Mm-hmm," I mumbled, wondering if he was real or if I'd slipped into a coma after that jackass raped me.

Maybe I'd slammed my head against the asphalt. I didn't feel it happen but then I wouldn't. I'd have been in a coma.

"I prefer blondes, though," he stated.

Lord, help me.

"You of course know," he began informatively, "that one of the most attractive things a woman can be is knowing exactly who she is, embracing that entirely, and not giving that first fuck what anyone thinks about it."

"You're freakin' me out," I informed him right back.

"Freak out in the car," he ordered, leaning into me, grabbing my hand, and dragging me out of the bathroom. "I skipped lunch. I'm starved."

I yanked on my hand when we were in my bedroom but he didn't let it go.

Though he did stop.

"You skipped lunch?" I asked.

"Yes," he answered.

"You shouldn't skip a meal, sugar. Your body *and* brain need nourishing regularly to take on the day. My guess, your line of business, you need to stay sharp. Losin' focus due to hunger pains don't say sharp."

Bizarrely, his reply came in a growl.

"You need to put your shoes on, get your bag, and get in my car, Daisy."

I again stared at him, doing it this time asking, "Pardon?"

"I'm trying to take this slow," he answered. "You being sweet is not conducive to me taking this slow."

Yep.

Right in the coochie.

"Oh," I mumbled.

"Yes. Oh. Get your shoes, your bag, and I'll meet you in the living room."

My head (and hair) nodded.

"Fuck me," he muttered, watching my hair move.

He squeezed my hand, let it go, and sauntered out of the room.

I got my shoes on, dropped my lip gloss in my bag, and met him there.

* * * *

"Tell me something good."

I was shifting the stem of the glass of my vodka martini this way and that with my red-tipped fingers.

We were at The Broker.

I'd been hither and yon since leaving home, all in the west, but I'd been in Denver for five years. The instant I hit the city limits, the Front Range spread out across the west as far as the eye could see, I knew it was the place where I'd die.

I'd always wanted to go to The Broker but I'd never been.

It was a date place. A special occasion place. A pricey place. A historic place. A place you went on a night you wanted to remember.

I didn't have many of those.

And there I was, sitting next to the handsomest man I'd ever seen, the kindest, the gentlest, and the most gentlemanly.

This last part in the last half hour Marcus had exercised greatly.

After we'd left my apartment, he'd opened the door of his black Mercedes for me (Ronald was not in attendance that evening; neither was Brady).

He'd opened it again to let me out of his Mercedes.

He'd also done the same when he'd let us in the building and he'd escorted me down the stairs and to our booth with his hand at the small of my back, light, warm, gallant.

He'd let me slide in first on the side I wanted, sliding in right beside me, and he'd asked me what I wanted to drink so he could order it for me when the waiter arrived.

He'd done the same with my meal.

I couldn't hack this.

I didn't know what to do with this.

It wasn't that this was a surprise.

It was just with what happened in that parking lot melting to take its place into a past with a lot of other stuff that wasn't all that great, precisely how it felt was only now hitting me.

And what that was, was the fact that Miss Annamae would adore Marcus Sloan.

She might look askance at whatever he did to be able to buy his Mercedes. But I had a feeling she'd overlook that simply with the way he'd murmured sweetly, "Watch your feet, darling," as I'd lifted them into his car.

"Daisy."

I turned my gaze from my glass to him.

He was watching me closely. "Are you all right?"

No.

And hell *yes.*

I didn't give him either of those answers.

I told him, "I've never been here."

"Excellent steaks," he murmured, still watching me closely.

"It's very nice."

Marcus made no reply.

"Did you, uh…" I tipped my head to the side, "ask me something?"

He turned more fully to me, shifting his bourbon and branch closer to the edge of the table in my direction, his long-fingered hand wrapped around it.

"I'd like you to tell me something good," he said.

"Okay," I replied readily and launched in. "You look real nice in that suit, sugar. And you got a good haircut. I like it."

His lips curled up. "Thank you, honey, but what I meant was, about you."

"About me?"

"About your life."

I tipped my head to the side even as I dipped and twisted my chin, my eyes drifting away from him.

"Please tell me it wasn't all bad."

He sounded like he really wanted me to do that so I looked at him and shared, "Momma had a man once. He was called Stretch. He called me sweetheart. He had broad shoulders, and even if they were fightin', any time his eyes came to me, he made them sweet. I thought it was like a superpower, him bein' all kinds a' mad at Momma, but bein' able to hide that from me. He used to ask me to go to my room, or if I was in my room, he'd come and close the door so I wouldn't see or hear them fightin'. It didn't work. But it sure was nice."

"Yes, that was nice," Marcus replied like it was but it wasn't.

The first part I knew was because at least Stretch had tried. The second was because there was fighting to shield me from.

I looked to my martini. "When he left, he told me I could call him whenever I needed him."

"That's nice too," Marcus said softly.

I looked to him. "He said it then kinda took it back 'cause Momma got up in his shit right while he was sayin' it. I remember it like it was yesterday and I was ten. But she was screamin' and carryin' on and shovin' him and he had no claim to me. I knew he wanted to try. I reckoned he liked me and he looked after me in his way when they were together, but he didn't want her in his life. He was done with her and I didn't blame him. She wasn't nice to him. She wasn't nice to anybody. She used him mostly to pay the cable bill and the electricity and whatever she could get outta him. I think he did it at first 'cause she was real pretty and he liked her coochie. Then he did it so I'd have cable and light because he just liked me. But to be done with her, I knew he knew, even if he didn't like it, he had to be done with me. So he left. And I never saw him again."

"That's not nice," Marcus rumbled, not appearing real thrilled at my story.

I shrugged, looked back to my martini, took in a deep breath and whispered my finish.

"Only man a' hers I missed when he was gone."

"That's all you have that's good?" he asked, not sounding real thrilled at that possibility.

I drew in another breath, and as I let it out, I looked back at Marcus and shared the real good stuff.

"For a spell, my momma worked as a daily girl for a lady named Miss Annamae. When I call her a lady, I mean she was a *lady*. A fine Southern woman who lived in a graceful mansion her beloved but sadly departed husband left to her after he died. A mansion he'd grown up in. So had his daddy and so on for a long while. He didn't rock her world with this. She grew up in one herself, just a different one from a different fine Southern family."

"You liked her," Marcus noted, still watching me closely.

"She liked me," I replied.

"I'm not thinking that's a good response," he muttered like he wasn't talking to me.

I let the stem of my glass go, turned more fully to him too, and reached out, putting my hand to his thigh.

When I did, I realized Marcus Sloan did not only take care of his grooming, he took care of other things too. The muscle beneath the fine material was solid.

My.

I tore my thoughts from what my hand was encountering, somehow found the strength to leave it right where it was, and told him, "She liked me. And she was kind to me. She gave me a tin of cookies she baked herself every Christmas my momma worked for her. And on my thirteenth birthday, she gave me an add-a-pearl necklace."

"That's very sweet," Marcus murmured.

I nodded. "It was."

"Did she add more pearls after your thirteenth?" he asked.

"She died three days after my birthday."

"Christ," he bit out low.

"And I hocked it for a bus ticket out of there when I was nineteen after I caught my boyfriend in the act, sleepin' with my best friend who was my best friend only to get to my boyfriend. I went direct home and told my momma all about it. I barely got the story out before she slapped me across the face and told me to get over it. Life was shit and then you died so no purpose wastin' it bitchin' about men bein' assholes when there wasn't a being with a penis who wasn't all asshole. And furthermore, I was a fool for havin' any friends. Women were backstabbers and man-stealers. They talked behind your back more than they said anything to your face but when they said somethin' straight to your face, if it was sweet, you could guarantee it was a lie."

"This isn't something good, Daisy," he informed me, not looking happy.

"It's all I got, Marcus," I told him but I gave his thigh a quick squeeze. "And it sounds bad. But Miss Annamae knew. She might not have known exactly what was gonna cut it but she knew somethin' would. And she knew I was a good girl. She knew I listened to her and she knew all the things she taught me I'd taken in. So she knew I'd need that necklace one day. Now, I think she mighta hoped that I'd wear it at my wedding to a wonderful man who'd help me fill my house with lots of babies. But I reckon she didn't hold a lot of hope for that and knew I'd need it for what I needed it for and she'd be happy I had it when I needed it and that it was her who gave it to me."

He kept hold of my gaze for a moment after I quit talking then he looked down at his drink and twisted it side to side in his fingers.

He looked reflective.

And upset.

And I didn't like that.

"Honey bunches of oats," I whispered.

His gaze came right back to mine.

And doing so, he made my heart warm right up in a way I knew sure as certain it would never again be cold.

Not ever.

Not ever again.

Not as long as Marcus was with me.

"It don't sound good but it was," I told him, real quiet, moved by his look that I felt in my heart. "I lost her but even though she'd been gone for years, she was there for me in that moment when I needed her most. It wasn't good for me there. And even with what happened to me in that parking lot, since I left that place, it's never again been that bad. That's how bad it was. She wanted me to have the means to escape when I'd had enough. It was the most precious gift anyone ever gave me. The time she gave it by handin' me that box. And the time I hocked it and bought myself freedom."

"There's no more good?" he asked.

"Smithie," I told him.

"Other than him."

"LaTeesha," I went on.

"Daisy, you understand me."

I shook my head and gave his thigh a squeeze. "Sugar, you aren't gettin' it. I had her for a short while. But I had her. Do you know where I'd be if I didn't?"

"No. Where would you be?"

"Back there in a place where every day was hell. I'd probably have a man who drank or gambled or shot up or beat me or all those. Or I'd have a string of 'em, none of 'em treatin' me right. A job that I hated workin', doin' it with people who thought they were better than me. My momma alternately hittin' me up for money or gettin' in my face, bein' ugly. Miss Annamae taught me to keep my head held high, darlin', and I was strugglin' with that." I leaned into him. "*Really* struggling. They would have beaten me. She gave me the way out when without her doin' that I'd have no way out, and here I am, in a fancy restaurant in a great town with a handsome man. It'd make her happy. Real happy, baby."

When I was done talking, his attention moved to my hair, as did his hand. He pulled some curls over my shoulder and stared at them resting there.

"You know why it was," he murmured to my hair.

"Pardon?"

His gaze came to mine and the hand he'd used to shift my hair he now used to sweep his fingertips across my cheekbone in a whisper of a touch that was there and gone.

But the precious memory of that touch would remain until the day I quit breathing.

"People live lives they hate," he said, resting his arm along the top of the booth beside me. "They see a patch of light, the only thing that drives them is to snuff it out."

I gave him a small smile and said, not mean, "That's sweet, sugar, but that's like tellin' a homely girl all the other girls bully her 'cause they're jealous."

"So what you're telling me is that all that's happened to you is just about predators preying on the weak?"

My head twitched.

"You aren't weak, Daisy," he stated.

No, I wasn't.

I'd been knocked down. Again and again.

I just kept getting up.

And I was still standing, in platforms, with great hair.

I swallowed.

"And those other girls bully the homely girl for one reason only. They're bitches. And that says a fuckuva lot more about them than that homely girl, and not one single bit of it is good."

My fingers tensed reflexively into his thigh.

"You're right, sugar," I whispered.

"I know," he returned. "As for you, why would a rich woman in a graceful mansion give the girl you thought you were the time of day?"

I felt the sting before I knew what was happening, and I blinked rapidly to keep them at bay.

Marcus didn't wait for me to answer.

He gave me *his* answer.

"Because she was old enough and lived enough life with enough abundance in that life to see you for what you were. Not a beautiful girl who would become a beautiful woman. Not a sweet girl who was strong and smart who would become so much more than her mother, it's laughable. Not a bold woman a weak man has to beat down to make him feel strong. Or fuck around on before she realizes she could do better and scrapes him off. No, she saw all of that, just without the bad shit leaking in."

I was now breathing deep along with blinking a lot in order to stop myself from losing it.

But even though Marcus saw it—I knew he even had to feel it— he was still far from done.

"I bet if you went back to that place, all those people would still be in it, living lives they hate. And you'd sweep through looking like a movie star and they'd take one look at you and know they had every right to be jealous of you. To hate you. To beat you. Talk about you. Cheat on you. And they're so entrenched in their bitterness because they only have themselves to blame that they didn't make their lives better, the only regret they'd have is that they hadn't been able to drag you right down to where they are, smother your light, make you go dark."

His fingers peeled mine from his thigh and curled around tight, holding my hand right there.

And he kept going.

"Miss Annamae didn't give you those pearls because she thought for a second they'd get close to beating you down. She gave you those pearls because she knew without a doubt they never would."

"Please stop talking," I whispered, seeing as he'd gone all fuzzy because my eyes were trembling with tears and I could take not one little bit more.

For a second, he didn't say anything and he didn't move.

Then he lifted my hand and touched his lips to my fingers. He put it right back, curling them around his thigh again, and he looked to his bourbon.

He raised his glass and took a sip.

I drew in a shaky breath.

Then I removed my hand from his thigh and reached for my own drink.

After I'd thrown back a slightly unladylike sip, I returned the glass to the table and my attention with it.

"Daisy."

"Please, *please*," I was still whispering, this time to my glass, "I can't take more of your sweet."

"Baby, you need to move your glass. Your appetizer is here."

My head came up.

The waiter smiled benignly at me.

I moved my glass.

Marcus moved his arm to around my back and pulled me to his side so I was tucked close.

I picked up my fork in order to dive into my crab cake.

I had the succulent-looking crab halfway to my mouth when Marcus asked, "Where did you grow up?"

I braced but answered, deciding that was an innocent enough question, and if he pressed for more, I'd shut it down.

He didn't press for more.

He scooped out some of his oysters Rockefeller.

And we ate.

* * * *

Marcus

Marcus got her drunk.

He did this without remorse.

It bought him a good deal of her amazing laughter.

It also got him the bonus of her passing out in his car, this meaning he didn't have to have words with her about where he fully intended to spend the night that night.

He carried her to her apartment and took off her shoes, her necklace, her bracelets, and carefully slid out her earrings but left her in her dress when he tucked her into bed.

He left her room, closing the door behind him at the same time sliding his phone out of the inside pocket of his suit jacket.

He flipped it open and made the call.

"Boss," Brady answered, sounding mostly alert, somewhat drowsy.

Within a minute, he'd issued his order.

He finished with, "Hopefully that pawn shop will still be open. If it isn't, maybe someone who ran it will be around and they kept records. But I don't care what it takes, Brady. Even if you have to pull Nightingale into it. Find those pearls and get them to me."

"You got it, Mr. Sloan."

"Goodnight," Marcus said and hung up.

Then he took off his suit jacket, his tie, shirt, shoes, and socks and he stretched out on Daisy's couch, tucking a toss pillow under his head and pulling one of her throws over his body.

He closed his eyes, and within seconds, with Daisy resting safe in the next room, Marcus was asleep.

Chapter Seven

Deal
Daisy

I opened my eyes and saw daisies.

Then I realized I was hungover.

On this realization, and the others that bounded in after it, in a tizzy, I pushed the covers down and saw I was in my dress from last night.

I touched my naked earlobe, felt my necklace gone, and looked back to the daisies to see my jewelry sitting at the base of the vase.

Then I turned, saw the other side of the bed was empty, stared at the fluffed pillows I hadn't slept on but grabbed one of them and pulled it to me to take a whiff.

It still smelled of Marcus, but this morning, only faintly.

He hadn't slept like I assumed he slept the night before, holding me.

He'd taken off.

I dropped to my back and closed my eyes in despair.

Wonderful.

I'd had a date the night before with the classiest man I'd ever met, and I got drunk, passed out in his car, and he'd had to put me to bed.

At least Marcus Sloan proved another way he was all class. He might have made sure I was comfortable, but he didn't give himself a show by taking my clothes off.

He also didn't stick around.

My hands balled into fists, my nails digging into the palms.

Because I was me, in the back of my mind, I knew if I was stupid enough to take a shot at the something special that was a man like Marcus Sloan, I'd screw it up with him and there I did it. The first date. I got shitfaced and I remembered laughing too much, being way too nosy asking too many questions, and doing that staring at him like every word he spoke dropped a bar of gold in my lap.

If drunken memory served, every time I laughed or touched his thigh, arm, or hand, he looked at me the same way.

I still passed out in his car, just like white trash.

And now he was gone.

"Ugh," I mumbled, the dull headache and subtle queasy feeling making it easier for me (just a touch) not to scream at my stupidity, find a way to kick my own ass (even mentally), or burst into tears.

Instead, since I was Daisy and from the moment I came out bawling I had no choice, I shoved the covers aside and got on with it.

I pushed myself out of bed, pulled my dress off on the way to the bathroom, and did my morning bathroom routine, this time adding the complicated procedure of getting all my makeup off.

My hair still rocked it since I rocked doing my hair, so I left it as is.

I went back into my room, tugged on a pair of baby-pink, drawstring, fleece shorts (that had diamanté sprinkled along the curves of the seams of the pockets) and a skintight white tank top that had emblazoned all across the front in hot-pink and glittery diamond rhinestones *Nothing a Little Sparkle Won't Fix*.

My mantra.

Though, that morning, post-fucking up my date with Marcus Sloan, I knew all the sparkle in the world wouldn't fix the feeling I had sitting in the pit of my belly that had nothing to do with being hungover.

I moved to my door in order to get water (for the aspirin I needed) and coffee (because every true red-white-and-blue American drank coffee), and find alternate ways to avoid the pain of a heart I refused to acknowledge I'd broken my damned self by acting like the white trash everyone thought I was.

I opened my door and stopped dead.

It was October, dead-on fall, and the sun hadn't yet hit the sky like only sun in Denver could, washing the base of a glorious mountain range in bright.

But the rising sun was doing its best lighting a room where every surface was covered with a spray of daisies. Some of them were pretty white ones with little yellow buttons in the middle. Others were white with green buttons. Some, a mixture of both. And others were pink. Or orange surrounding the black button blazing out to a startling yellow. Others were red. Then there were those that were coral. There were also those with color combinations.

On a routine basis, I carefully clipped their ends, added fresh water with food, all in an effort to keep them alive as long as I could.

Over the weeks, I'd had to throw some away.

But they were of a quality that most of them were still going strong.

And right then, in the midst of them, lying on his stomach on my couch, one long arm having fallen off the side, my throw having slid down to his waist, the delineation of the muscles of his tanned back on show, his head turned from me resting on a toss pillow, his thick dark hair disheveled, lay Marcus.

He hadn't left the drunken, stripping floozy who'd passed out in his Mercedes in her bed and taken off.

Like a gentleman, when she wasn't in the throes of a trauma, he'd slept on the couch.

I looked at him, his long body stretched out amongst the daisies, asleep, but having stayed close so he could make sure I was safe, safe from anything, even nightmares, and I made a noise in the back of my throat I couldn't control.

When I did, I watched his body twitch then he came up on his forearms and his sleepy blue eyes turned my way.

He looked ready to move further but he caught himself when he saw me.

I stared into his eyes, knowing I probably made noise getting up, doing my thing in the bathroom, getting dressed.

But it was my quiet sob that had woken him.

Marcus Sloan.

God, *he killed me.*

I leaned my shoulder against the doorjamb, drawing in breath through my nose, controlling the tears with some effort, taking more time to swallow them back.

After another breath, watching him watching me unmoving, I spoke.

"You know what got me through?"

"Baby," he whispered but still didn't move. He just lay there on his stomach, up on his forearms, his head turned to me, his eyes glued to me, just like he knew that's what I needed him to do.

Just that. Stay on my couch and let me say what I needed to say.

"Thought I was nothing," I shared softly.

He pushed up, the muscles in his biceps bulging, threw off the blanket, and turned to sit on his ass.

He hadn't taken off his trousers.

That couldn't be a comfortable way to sleep.

But a gentleman in a lady's home got as comfortable as he could get, but unless he was invited to do it, he didn't take off his trousers.

Lord.

Marcus Sloan.

"Proved it to me, that guy," I told him. "Raping me. The world had been givin' me signs since I was born. But he proved it to me."

"I need you to come here," Marcus requested gently.

I ignored him and kept going.

"Told myself that. Was certain of it, at first. The thing was, if I was nothing, why was someone sending me daisies?"

That cut it for him.

He started to push up.

Quickly, I asked, "Please. Don't. Please let me finish."

He settled, gaze locked to me, and he showed me with his expression that he didn't like it but he kept his place.

For me.

"So pretty," I whispered. "So bright and happy. They were everywhere. I wanted to think dark thoughts. I wanted to cut myself down. I just couldn't keep it up. And it wasn't Miss Annamae this time who helped me see what it was important to see."

"Darling—"

I'd beat them away but they came right back and I knew it when the bead of cold wet slid down my cheek.

"It was you," I finished.

"Daisy, I need to come to you."

No he didn't.

I needed to go to him.

And that was what I did, scared—no, terrified.

But slowly, one foot in front of the other, I did it, and he watched me every step of the way.

And when I got just a little bit close, he bent way forward. His long arms coming right out, his fingers grasped me at my hips and pulled me into his lap.

Then he kissed me.

It was soft and it was sweet.

But it was more.

The tip of his tongue touched my lips and I instantly let him inside. He swept in, his arms around me closing tighter. He twisted at his waist, leaned into me, and I felt my back hit the couch, the warmth of his broad chest pressing to mine, his hand diving in my curls and closing around my scalp.

I had my arms around his shoulders, one hand curved tight around the back of his neck, and I kissed him back trying to come even a little bit close to giving him back all he'd given me.

Daisies.

Lobster.

Laughter.

Patience.

Understanding.

Everything.

I pressed my breasts into his chest.

He groaned, then growled into my mouth, but I felt it in my coochie, and he took the kiss deeper. One of his arms curving down, his hand gliding down my side, his trajectory I knew to my ass.

But before he got there, that arm locked tight around my waist, his lips slid from mine to my neck and he kissed me there.

Then he held me that way, his warm breath coming fast against my neck, all the other warmth of his hard body pressed to me.

I didn't get it.

So I called, "Marcus?"

"Taking this slow," he answered a question I didn't exactly ask and he sounded like it was the last thing he wanted to do, not just saying it, doing what he said.

That was sweet. I was sure I needed it.

Still.

"You coulda maybe taken second base," I shared.

His head came up, his twinkling eyes caught mine, and he was smiling.

"Maybe next time."

"Look forward to that," I mumbled.

"Now I'm going to make you breakfast."

I frowned and asked, "Whose apartment is this?"

"Yours," he answered, still smiling.

"So rules are, I have a drama, the morning after, you can make me breakfast. I don't have a drama, which, honey bunches of oats, I'm hopin' to be drama-free for a good long while, I make breakfast. *Comprende?*"

I knew what I was saying.

But more, *he* knew it.

And he liked it.

A whole lot.

"Deal," he replied, eyes still twinkling.

"Do you like pancakes?" I asked.

"Yes," he answered.

I squinted at him. "Got a load of your six-pack, sugar."

And I had. His chest and stomach were better than his back. Well, not really, it was just that I didn't mind losing the sight of his back if I had his chest and abs to look at. Or his shoulders. Or his face.

"Daisy."

On my name, he sounded like he was laughing.

I stopped thinking about his chest (and other things) and focused on him.

Yep.

Laughing.

Pull yourself together, girl!

"Sorry," I muttered then rallied. "So, if I make you pancakes, will your body rebel and I'll have to take you to the hospital? Or will you have to eat nothing but celery for two weeks to make up for it?"

"I cooked in your kitchen, honey," he reminded me. "I didn't notice many healthy options."

"I'm Southern. If it isn't fried, griddled, or grilled, it's grilled, griddled, or fried. We might get up to some boilin', but only if it's crawfish, lobster, or shrimp, and I don't have none of that." I hesitated, making a mental grocery list before I concluded, "Right now."

"I'm thinking I'll have to add another hour to my workout every day if you're doing the cooking."

My eyes got big.

"You work out *every day?*"

His body shook against mine with his laughter and his word shook with it too, "Yes."

"That explains it," I muttered.

"Daisy?"

I focused again on him and not the delicious vision of him working out.

"Yeah?"

"You have a beautiful body, too."

I smiled. "Thanks, sugar, that's sweet."

"You're welcome, darling," he said warmly. "But what I'm saying is, you have that body. You also have three packets of bacon, and only because I cooked up the last of the opened one yesterday, so before, you had three and a half."

"This is true," I confirmed, like having four packets of bacon (and I made another mental note for my grocery list that I was one down) was the most natural thing in the world.

Because it was.

"And you don't work out?" he asked then added with his arms giving me a squeeze, "Every day?"

"I strip. Then I practice strippin'. Then I help the other girls practice strippin', doin' it by showin' them some good moves." I paused before I finished, "And I power walk."

"Ah," he murmured.

"I also have to cart around these bazungas," I shared, deciding not to take my arm from around him (because I liked my arms around him) in order to gesture to said bazungas he couldn't exactly miss since he was lying on them. "And that burns some calories, believe you me."

He was still murmuring, and his eyes were still twinkling, when he said, "I bet."

It was then I decided to remove an arm from around him but only so I could put a hand to his jaw and rub my thumb over the dark stubble on his cheek.

It rasped against the pad of my thumb and felt nice.

Real nice.

And I watched the twinkle in his eye disappear but only so he could replace it with something I liked just as much.

I kept doing this with my thumb as I said softly, "I need some aspirin, baby. I got me a little hangover from last night and it's all good with you lookin' hot on my couch and bein' hot while kissin' me then bein' sweet while talkin' about pancakes. But that's settin' in again so I gotta get on doin' something about it and then feedin' my hot guy."

"You have an extra toothbrush?"

My eyes rolled back to study my bangs for a second as I mentally inventoried my bathroom drawers then I looked at him again and said, "Yeah."

"You get me that. I'll get you the water and aspirin. Then you can start cooking."

I grinned at him.

"Deal."

* * * *

We were sitting at my dinette and I was shoveling in pancakes while envisioning the dining room table I was going to buy when I got my new place (this in an effort not to envision what Marcus's shoulders looked like under the shirt he'd put back on—he was fine in that shirt—he was finer out of it).

Marcus was shoveling in pancakes too. Though, he was classier about it.

"How'd you get all classy?" I asked.

"Sorry?" he asked back.

I circled my fork with its hunk of pancakes dripping syrup at him.

"You said you didn't have much growin' up. Your daddy played the ponies. Your sister was a stripper. But you look and act like a Kennedy, except hotter, and without forgettin' how to pronounce your R's."

"Got a job at a country club to help my sister out when I was fourteen," he shared.

I nodded.

"Some of the adults were all right. The rest acted like I didn't exist. The kids were jackasses."

"I've got no doubt," I murmured, watching him like a hawk.

"I belong to that country club now."

His words socked me right in the chest in a very happy way.

Real slow, I felt a smile spread on my face.

"You knew what you wanted, you made it happen."

He gave one nod. "Exactly."

I'd made a decision. I was scared to death of it. But I'd made it and I'd shared it with Marcus.

It was time to get to the important stuff.

"You want babies, sugar?" I asked quietly.

"Yes."

I let out the breath I hadn't realized I'd been holding after I asked my question and before I asked another one.

"How many?"

"As many as my wife will let me make."

Excellent answer.

"Do you want them, Daisy?"

"Yes."

"How many?"

"As many as my man will let me make."

We sat there, not eating, just staring at each other.

I broke the silence by giving him the honesty.

"Just sayin', darlin', this takin' it slow is not real easy."

His eyes heated but his face went soft.

"Let me take care of you," he whispered.

I didn't know. I couldn't keep up. He gave me a lot of it.

But in that moment, those words felt like the sweetest Marcus had ever given to me.

I pressed my lips together, rolled them, and nodded.

"I like it that you don't want slow but you need it, baby," he went on.

He was probably right about that, even if after that kiss on my couch that morning, I wanted him to be wrong.

I didn't offer him these thoughts.

I just kept nodding.

"Dinner tonight, my house," he decreed. His lips curled up slightly. "Since it's my house, I'm cooking for you, honey." The lip curl went away as his tone grew firm. "And I want you to bring a bag but I'm sleeping in the guest room and you're not."

What could I do?

I'd made a decision. And Marcus knew that decision.

And on the other point, it *was* his house. Maybe one day (I hoped, please God, did I hope) I could horn in and do what a good woman should do for her man, that being the cooking (and I didn't think on what Marcus and his six-pack had in his fridge—I was Southern, I could eat a strawberry if it was on the bottom of a champagne glass and some Brussels sprouts if they were coated in bacon grease, but that's about as far as it went).

But right then, I had one choice.

And for once in my life, it was a good choice.

So I again nodded.

"Eat," he ordered. "I need to get to work."

I just kept nodding.

He gave me a sweet smile.

And then we both ate.

Chapter Eight

Just a Dream
Daisy

That evening, I sat next to Marcus in the back of his big limousine, Ronald driving (again wearing sunglasses, seriously, and night had fallen and everything!), Brady sitting next to him in the front, Marcus sitting next to me with his fingers fiddling with mine against his thigh.

He was on his phone.

It had been a surprise when Brady, not Marcus, had collected me at my door, taking my bag and also putting his hand to the small of my back as he escorted me to the car.

When Brady opened the door to let me in, Marcus was on the phone but his gaze was on me.

However, the instant I sat my ass next to him, he muttered into his cell, "I need a moment."

He didn't wait for whoever he was talking to to give him that moment.

He put his hand over the bottom half of his phone, leaned into me, brushed my lips with his, then slanted his head and kissed my neck.

He pulled away and said, "I'm sorry, honey. This is important. I'll try not to let it take too long."

I'd just had my man's man collect me from my door, carry my

bag, guide me chivalrously to a limousine in the back of which was *my man.*

He could be on the phone for an hour, two. With all that and the way he greeted me and apologized, I didn't give a shit.

To communicate this, I smiled at him, nodded, settled my ass into the leather and it was then he took my hand, pulled it to his thigh, and started fiddling with my fingers.

We drove from my building that was on the east side of Cherry Creek past Colorado Boulevard, into downtown.

It took Marcus all that time to wind down his phone call and he only flipped his cell shut when Ronald hit the indicator and made a turn into underground parking.

"Sorry, darling," Marcus murmured and I turned my head to him. "How was your day?"

"I watched *Gone with the Wind, Cat on a Hot Tin Roof,* and *Fried Green Tomatoes,* so I'm topped up in Southern diva goodness."

He grinned. "Does that ever run low?"

I shook my head (and hair—I'd gone with my Farrah Fawcett flips-waves-and-curls-run-amuck-except-bigger look), but said, "I'm not takin' any chances."

His grin became a smile. He tugged on my hand and pulled me in so he could touch his lips to my forehead.

About that time, Ronald pulled into a spot and stopped, so I tore my eyes from Marcus's retreating lips and looked out the windshield.

There was a big sign on the concrete wall in front of the spot that said, *RESERVED. PENTHOUSE.*

Uh.

Penthouse?

The door at my side opened and Marcus let my hand go to put his to my hip and give it a light shove, encouraging in a murmur, "Let's get you fed, baby."

I slid out.

That was when I saw in front of the three spots next to the limousine, one that held Marcus's Mercedes, one that held a black Escalade, and since the Escalade was so big I didn't see what the other one held, but I did see the same sign on the wall that was in front of the limo and the other spots.

Four parking spaces.

All his.

My Lord.

Marcus took my hand and led me to the elevator that was *right next* to the parking spot the limo was in.

But of course the owner of the penthouse would have all the best spots.

The elevator came. We got in. Brady got in with us. Ronald and his sunglasses did too.

And it was Ronald that tapped in a code on the elevator pad then hit the button that had the letters PH.

They stood in front of us.

We stood at the back.

I looked up at Marcus. "You said you had a condo."

He looked down at me. "I do."

"A condo *penthouse?*"

He grinned again and squeezed my hand.

"Lobster, limos, and penthouses. You're somethin', sugar," I muttered.

"I'll take that as good," he replied.

I looked to the backs of the boys in front of me, stating, "Seein' as that's how I meant it, you go right ahead."

At that, he let my hand go but only so he could curve his arm around my waist and curl me so my front was pressed to his side.

I looked up at him again. "This is a long ride, darlin'. Your penthouse on the moon?"

With that, he burst out laughing.

And I loved every second of it, hearing it and watching it.

Unfortunately, in the middle of it, the elevator doors opened.

We walked out into a plush little hallway that had an armchair and a table with a lamp on it over which was a mirror, all this for reasons I didn't know since you needed a code to get to that floor so I suspected no one would be hanging there waiting for Marcus to get home.

It also had a big, gleaming wooden door that had to be a foot bigger than normal doors *on every side*. This had a shining brass door handle that would fit a manor house, except it was snazzier.

Marcus walked us to it, but didn't fit a key into the door. He slid aside the door over a panel on the wall I hadn't even noticed and entered another code.

I heard the lock unlatch.

He opened the door and positioned me to move through it with his hand at my back, saying to the boys, "Tomorrow."

"Yes, boss," I heard Brady say.

Ronald wasn't a big talker, apparently, since he again said nothing.

"Later, boys," I called, looking over my shoulder at them as Marcus pressed me in.

Brady grinned at me. Ronald just stared at me through his apparently ever-present sunglasses.

Marcus shut the door.

My gaze went to Marcus and I saw Brady had handed off my bag to him.

"Does Ronald not like me?"

He got close. "Ronald likes beer, brats, Broncos, and busty women, not in that order. He hasn't shared, but if I had to guess, my guess would be he loves you."

That was good but I wasn't sure it was true.

"Brady seems friendly," I noted. "Ronald, not so much."

"Brady is friendly because that's part of Brady being Brady. Ronald is old school, and as far as he's concerned, he isn't paid to be friendly. Especially not to any woman I'd bring dinner to or have sitting next to me in my car."

I tipped my head to the side. "How many of those are there?"

"In my car, enough. Bringing dinner to, one."

I smiled.

He smiled back and got closer. "I'm going to change. Then I'll show you around. After that, I'll start dinner."

"Sounds like a plan."

"Make yourself at home," he invited, lifted his hand, touched my nose, then turned and sauntered up some stairs, carrying my bag with him.

That was when I noticed the stairs.

They swept at a curve off to the side of the entry and they had an elegantly carved bannister the likes I'd never seen. All whorls and swirls, it was amazing. And the treads of the stairs were covered with a thick, opulent carpet in the color of the palest mushroom.

Beyond that, I took in floor-to-ceiling windows with an uninterrupted view of the Front Range. Uninterrupted except for the elegant drape of oyster-colored curtains pulled back at the sides.

And in the space just beyond the staircase, on gleaming parquet floors, sat a table with a massive spray of delicate butterscotch-colored flowers, the type I didn't know, these rising up from a huge crystal vase. Two curved, elegant chairs sat at angles to the table for no reason whatsoever, except to look posh, seeing as no one would sit there unless Marcus was throwing a big party.

I hadn't even walked in and I knew his place wasn't class.

It was *class*.

He had all this.

He could come from living a life that was close to squalor and build a life where this was what he saw when he got home.

And he'd picked me.

Me.

He'd not only picked me, he'd said he'd waited thirty-five years for me.

So I stood just inside his door and I did this not feeling uncomfortable.

I felt for the only time in my life outside the time I hit the Denver city limits like I was right where I was supposed to be.

What I wasn't going to do was make myself at home.

No, I reckoned if the entry was that fabulous, the rest was going to blow my mind.

And I wanted to experience it with Marcus.

So I didn't leave the entry. I walked to the windows, stared out at the Front Range, and waited for him to come back.

"Honey, I told you to make yourself at home."

I turned to see Marcus coming down the final wind to the stairs wearing another pair of nice jeans, these topped with a garnet-colored sweater with a handsome, manly shawled collar.

"I didn't want to experience your place without you with me," I told him.

A look passed his face right before he got in my space.

I didn't have a chance to figure out what the look meant seeing as a nanosecond after he got in my space, I was in his arms and he was kissing me.

And that kiss was another doozy, slightly less of one than what he gave me that morning, seeing as we were standing up and we both had on more clothes (well, Marcus did, I had on a pair of faded jeans with strategically-placed worn spots (a lot of them), high-heeled, gray leather cowboy boots with turquoise ostrich feathers stitched in, and a silvery off-the-shoulder sweater that held on to my boobs by a miracle, so not more clothes, exactly, just more coverage, kind of).

The kiss was still a doozy.

When he lifted his head, I was having trouble breathing and I was holding on to his shoulders because my legs had gone weak.

"Want a tour?" he whispered.

Hell yes, I wanted a tour.

Though I'd prefer another kiss.

Horizontal again this time.

I didn't share that.

I nodded.

He grinned.

Then he let me go, took my hand, and gave me a tour.

And we'll just say I was right.

The entry was pure class.

The rest of it was like a dream.

* * * *

"I'm having Kelly clear my schedule so next week we can go to my place in Aspen."

I sat at his side at his impressive dining room table where he sat at the head, a fork with linguine wrapped around its tines, Marcus's homemade buttery, garlicky clam sauce dripping off it halfway to my mouth, and I looked to him.

There was a lot there. I didn't know where to start.

So I started with the easiest part.

"Kelly?" I asked, then shoved the pasta into my mouth.

"My PA," he answered, reaching to the bottle of sauvignon blanc that was in a silver bucket filled with ice on the table (yes, Marcus had a silver wine bucket, making me think that perhaps he *had it all* and I wasn't talking about shit you could buy, just *it all*).

He refilled my wine while I asked my next.

"You have a place in Aspen?"

He put the bottle back and his eyes came to me as he replied, "Yes."

I twirled linguine. "What else you got?"

"A beach house on Coronado. And a set of six lots that I bought in Englewood four years ago that had houses on them that were in a great neighborhood, but not in great shape. I had them razed and then had a number of trees planted so when the time came for me to build there I'd be in the city, close to work, but I'd have nature around me, peace, quiet, and privacy."

A beach house in Coronado.

Nice.

And peace, quiet, and privacy.

That sounded *real* good.

"Mm-hmm," I muttered to my linguine before I put it into my mouth.

"Does that trouble you?"

I chewed, swallowed, and answered, "Why would it trouble me?"

"You seem troubled," he remarked.

I put my fork on my plate and gave him my full attention.

"I'm not troubled that evidence is suggesting you're a lot more loaded than I thought you were, and I thought you were pretty loaded, sugar." I said my next watching him carefully, which was the same way I was speaking, "I'm troubled because you wanna take me to Aspen next week when I'm gonna be back at work."

His head tipped a bit to the side, but other than that he didn't look ticked.

However, he did ask, "You're going back to work?"

"Yes."

"So soon?"

"It's not soon, honey bunch," I told him cautiously. "By the time I go back, I'll have been on vacation for a month."

That got me a scary look as his eyes went hard.

"You weren't on vacation, Daisy."

"I've been away," I said quietly. "And I'm a draw. I'm not on that stage, they don't need the rope outside and the only person who doesn't hurt because of that is me, seein' as Smithie has me on paid leave and he pays me a whack. But you know that, I'm sure."

He inclined his head and kept his gaze on me. "I do."

"So I need to get back to work." I shot him a smile. "And anyway, I'm runnin' out of Southern movies to watch. *The Divine Secrets of the Ya-Ya Sisterhood* is a kickass book, but the movie sucks."

Marcus reached for his bread, murmuring, "I'll talk to Smithie. He can wait a week while we're in Aspen, and when we come back, if you still want to dance, you can go back then."

I didn't get into the "if you still want to dance" part.

I said, "I already arranged it with Smithie, Marcus."

He chewed his bread, swallowed, and locked his eyes on me. "I'll rearrange it."

Oh boy.

"Okay, sugar, just to say, that's my job and Smithie's my boss. I know you got a stake in that club but *he's* my boss, and we got it arranged."

"And like I'll said, I'll rearrange it."

"I got a Porsche to pay for."

"And you're on paid leave." He shook his head and took up his fork. "It's too soon."

"Honey, I need to get back to life. I had my time. I got my daisies. I did my drama. I'm not sayin' nothin' else is gonna spring up with all that and bite me in the ass. I'm gonna have my moments. But now, sittin' around the house is one long moment that reminds me my life was interrupted by that asshole."

"You won't be thinking about that in Aspen with me."

"True enough," I agreed. "And I wanna do that, Marcus. I really do. I've never been to Aspen and I bet it's real pretty. And it's sweet you wanna spend time with me there. It's just sweet you like spending time with me. But Smithie takes care of me. It's time I take care of him right back. Maybe after a while, I can take a few days and we can go."

"Smithie's fine, Daisy."

"Without me there, Smithie's bleeding money, Marcus."

"He isn't."

"Maybe you don't get to look at the books but when I say he pays me a whack, he pays me *a whack*."

His gaze steady on me, he socked it to me.

"He doesn't. I do. I cover your salary, Daisy, and I have for the last two months."

"Say what?" I whispered.

"I pay your salary. Smithie couldn't afford you."

But I was stuck on the *last two months.*

The last two months.

The last two months where that time ago Smithie took away a whole set, one song off the other sets and ended my lap dances but increased my pay so much, my eyeballs burned when I got a good look at the first paycheck.

And...

Two months.

Before the rape.

Before *anything.*

"Say what?" I repeated, not on a whisper, on a breath.

"I didn't want you on the stage for four sets with those sets being three songs, too long alone up there and exposed. And I *definitely* didn't want you doing lap dances. So to cover the loss in tips that would be, we elevated your salary, and because Smithie couldn't pay that and it wasn't his decision, I covered it."

"You didn't know me."

"No. But I knew I wanted to."

I stared at him.

Then I started, "Why didn't you—?"

I cut myself off because it felt all of a sudden like something was stuck in my throat and I thought it pertinent to focus on breathing.

"Daisy?"

Marcus looked concerned.

I put a hand flat on the table and pushed through the thing choking me.

"That was two months ago."

"Darling—"

"Before he got to me."

Marcus went still.

I pushed up on my hand, shoved back my seat, and took my feet.

"*Why didn't you come to me?*" I screeched.

He was out of his seat, too, and approaching me.

"Daisy—"

I scuttled back and lifted up a hand but he didn't stop moving so I didn't either as I bit out, "Don't come near me."

"I had things happening," he said quietly.

"You saw me. You knew you wanted to take your shot," I hissed. It all was coming to me, pouring over me like boiling oil. "That day. That day you were there and you left without even looking at me. You were up in Smithie's office with Smithie. The next day Smithie gave me my raise. You saw me. You knew then."

He kept coming at me, stalking me around the table.

"When I made my approach, Daisy, I wanted it to have my full attention."

"If I was Marcus Sloan's moll, no one would even think of touching me."

"I couldn't have known you'd be raped, baby."

I shook my head, still retreating while he advanced and he did it speaking.

"And you're wrong. Men like that I don't get so I don't get how they can do the things they do, but if he had that monstrousness in his head, it's doubtful anyone could have stopped him, even me."

He was making sense and I didn't need sense.

"I need to go," I forced out.

"It's not my fault."

That made me stop dead. The words and the tortured way he said them.

When I stopped, he moved in. Hands cupping the sides of my head, he held it back and bent his face to mine.

"It's not my fault, honey. It isn't anyone's fault. If I could have stopped it, I would. If I could make a miracle and go back in time to erase it, I would. But I can't. And you could have been mine then, and unless I had reason to put a man on you, which I can't say I would do, not in the beginning, it might alarm you and I would do nothing that might alarm you, he would have found his way to get to you."

I shook my head in his hands then nodded it.

"You're right."

He stared into my eyes.

"I'm…I…I'm…"

"Just take a breath," he urged.

I did that.

Then I said it.

"I'm sorry." I shoved my head through his hands so I could plant my face in his chest and I grabbed onto his sweater at the sides of his waist. "God, I'm so sorry."

He wrapped his arms around me, murmuring into the top of my hair, "It's okay."

I let his sweater go so I could wrap my arms around him too.

Marcus held me and I held him back.

Eventually, still in my hair, he said softly, "Thinking this is one of those moments you were talking about."

"Yeah," I muttered, embarrassed, so I shoved my face deeper into his chest. "God, I'm so, *so* sorry."

"Don't apologize."

I tipped my head back. "That was…it was stupid. It wasn't even logical."

"You get a pass on being illogical. At least for another month or six or, seeing as you're female, another seventy years."

I narrowed my eyes at him.

He grinned down at me.

His grin faded, his look grew probing, and he whispered, "Good?"

I stopped giving him the stink eye and nodded. "Yeah, honey."

"Go to Aspen with me."

"And the hot guy takes advantage," I muttered.

His grin came back. "I didn't get where I am pissing away opportunities either, Daisy."

I rolled my eyes.

He gave me a light shake.

I rolled them back.

"Aspen," he pushed.

"I need to take care of Smithie."

He studied me.

Then he sighed.

It took a lot but I didn't smile my triumph, just felt it warm me deep down inside.

But I got serious when I asked, "You pay me?"

"Yes."

"Is that…uh, gonna continue?"

"Do you like stripping?"

"I'm fucking amazing on that stage."

He shook his head, but did it with his lips curled up, holding me tight. "Then yes, it'll continue as long as you want to be on that stage."

"I rocked a private dance, sugar, but I can't say they were my favorite things. They were just below having my eyes burned out with a red-hot fire poker, having my nails ripped out at the roots, and having a really bad hair day."

He started chuckling.

It looked good on him but I didn't join in.

When Marcus noticed my seriousness, he sobered and asked, "What?"

"There's nothing I can ever—"

He let me go with one hand to put two fingers to my lips.

When I shut up, he took his fingers away and said, "Something else my sister taught me. If you can give it, you don't blink at giving someone you care about something they need or they want. No matter how deep it cuts, how much it costs, how steep the price might be in a different way. It's an honor and it's a blessing. So giving you the things I can give you means I'm honored and blessed, Daisy. Please don't take that away from me."

I stared up at him thinking Marcus Sloan wasn't like a dream.

He was just a dream.

And on that thought, I blurted, "Miss Annamae would love you."

Again, something new moved over his face and I held my breath at its splendor.

"Consider me paid back," he whispered.

Lord.

He.

Was.

Killing.

Me!

"Oh my God!" I snapped. "You're gonna make me cry again."

"Cry in your linguine, darling, it's getting cold," he returned, pulling me to his side and guiding me back to my chair.

I sat.

He sat.

Then I groused, "Who woulda thought some asshole cheatin' on me or beatin' on me would be easier to take than some hot guy *honored* and *blessed* to spoil me rotten."

"You'll get used to it," Marcus murmured to his linguine.

I stared at his dark head bent over his plate right along with feeling my heart contract.

He lifted that head, swallowed, and asked, "What?"

"I don't know whether to throw something at you or jump you."

He grinned a wicked grin that set my coochie to buzzing.

"We're taking it slow, remember?"

"Yeah. Right. Great."

He kept grinning and the buzzing got stronger.

"Stop turning me on," I warned.

"Stop being cute," he fired back.

I stuck my tongue out at him.

He watched it then looked in my eyes. "That didn't work."

"Whatever," I muttered, grabbed my bread, and gnawed off a huge chunk with my teeth.

Marcus burst out laughing.

And I loved the sound.

Whatever!

* * * *

Marcus ripped his mouth from mine, rested his forehead against mine, and murmured a labored, "Christ."

I stood pressed against the doorjamb of his bedroom, my chest heaving, brushing against his, this setting my nipples to tingling (or setting them to tingling *more*). My fingers were also gripping the back of his sweater in a way that I was sure would misshape it forever.

It was a great sweater. This would be a shame.

I just couldn't find it in me at that minute to care.

It was time to go to bed.

And Marcus led me to his bedroom, where I was sleeping (and he would hear none of it that I could take a guest room (he didn't have one like he'd said, he had *three*) so I shut up about it) and he'd just given me a goodnight kiss that led to another one that led to another one that led to a make-out session in his doorway.

He had one hand curled around the back of my neck, the other hand braced on the jamb over my head.

His hold and pose were hot.

So I was not feeling slow.

At all.

"I think maybe we can—" I began.

He lifted his forehead from mine and cut me off.

"We need to work up to it."

"I'm up for more working up to it," I shared with him breathily.

He took his hand from the jamb and brushed his fingers along my jaw.

"Don't make this harder," he ordered gently.

I wanted to make something harder.

To communicate this, I replied, "I know ways to make it a whole lot easier."

"Daisy, honey, you lost it at dinner."

Damn.

"We need to work up to it," he repeated.

He was right.

And that stunk.

"All right," I grumbled.

"All right," he replied sweetly.

"Can we make a deal that if I have forty-eight hours drama-free, you'll consider banging me?"

He smiled down at me. "Honey, I'm never going to *bang you*. What we're going to do will not including banging."

I didn't know what to make of that.

"What're we gonna do?" I asked, not to get a rise out him (in that way, or any way).

I was curious.

"We're not going to bang."

"Okay, so what're we gonna do?"

"You bang someone you give a gold bracelet to to say good-bye when you've lost interest in banging her. The man I am does not bang a woman like you."

Oh Lord.

His brows drew together as he watched my face. "Are you going to cry again?"

"No," I snapped, though I was feeling close to it. So I needed a retreat, stat. "Go away. I need to crawl into your huge-ass bed, smell you on your sheets, and fight the desire to ask you to let it be *me* who puts a bullet into that jackass's forehead."

"That isn't going to happen."

I blinked at the sudden change in the tone of his voice.

It wasn't just firm.

It was steel grating against steel.

"I was just joshin'," I told him carefully.

"Well, I'm not. I do what I do. I have other concerns that I'm growing alongside those you don't know about, you'll never know about, but know they're there. I do this to assure the future I intend to have. That's the part of my life where you'll have your place. The *only* part. This gets done, you live in that light. I never put you in any dark."

"Okay, sugar," I soothed, because I needed to soothe. The sparks flying off his steel were singeing me.

The heat went out of his gaze, he bent and touched his mouth to mine, and then he gave my neck a squeeze.

He did all this right before he didn't play fair.

"Now, go to bed, baby. And if you do something while you're wrapped up in my sheets that I'd love, but right now knowing you were doing it would kill me, please be quiet. I intend to be."

My eyes got huge.

His got wicked.

Then he brushed his lips against mine again, took his time trailing his hand from my neck so his fingers went all the way through my hair before he stepped away and walked away, not looking back.

Still, I watched until he disappeared through a door down the hall.

Okay, giving you the honesty.

I watched his ass until it disappeared through a door down the hall.

But there was some shoulder watching too.

I closed the door to his room, got ready for bed, and for the first time since what happened to me happened to me, I took care of business wrapped up in Marcus's sheets.

And really, who could blame me?

Not to mention, he'd totally primed me so it was *awesome*.

And not once did I think about what had happened to me.

Oh no.

After I took care of myself as quiet as I could, I rolled over, smelled Marcus, closed my eyes with a smile on my face, and slept like a baby.

Chapter Nine

Love Boat
Daisy

I sat with my bare feet up on a chair in the dressing room at Smithie's, a cold Fat Tire beer in my hand.

The beer was not my choice. It was Wynter's birthday. She wanted a tub filled with Fat Tire, so Smithie left one for us in the dressing room. Though it wasn't my choice, it was the first time I'd ever had it and that beer was *yum*.

My contribution was a big birthday sheet cake practically covered with huge frosting roses.

Oh, and the cake also had the words *Happy Birthday, Wynter!* and the whole thing was covered in edible glitter dust.

I was sipping and grinning at Chardonnay, who was telling a story.

"So then I was all, 'What's your problem?' And she was all, '*I* don't have a problem. What's *your* problem?' And I was all, 'Do you see me talking to this guy?' And she was all, 'Whatever.' And I was all, '*Not* whatever. You just came up to him while I was talking to him and shoved your tits in his face.' And she was all, 'I did not do that.' And I was all, 'I got eyes in my head, don't I?' And then the guy says, 'You did do that. And it was *not* cool. I'm talking to her.'" Her face got dreamy and so did her voice when she finished, "His name was Dylan, and he was fine."

Then she gave me big eyes.

"How fine, sugar bunch?" I asked.

She lifted her hands and held her pointed fingers out at least ten inches. *"Fine."*

That was when *my* eyes got big. "That *is* fine."

"So what happened with this chick?" Ashlynn asked.

"She bitchslapped her," Paris put in. "I was there. It was fucking *aces.*"

"Good for you," I said to Chardonnay.

"You got *that* right, sister," Chardonnay replied.

We giggled.

"Know this chick," Paris said into our giggles, grabbing up a handful of the cashews that Ashlynn brought, which, as far as I was concerned, seriously classed up a birthday party in a stripper dressing room. Then again, cashews classed up anything. "Her name is Dawn. She's so good spreadin' her bitch around, think she's goin' for the world record of bitchdom."

Then she threw back the cashews.

"Dawn?" China sidled up, pulling out her own Fat Tire and reaching for the opener. "I think I know her. She went after my girl Bethany's man. He is *hot.*" Her face got distracted. "Though I think she's just a booty call. His name is Hawk. And that night when that Dawn chick made her move was the only time he's been seen with her in public and that's only because he was pickin' her up from this party so he could have his booty call."

"This dude's name is Hawk?" Chardonnay asked.

China nodded.

"Who's called Hawk?" Chardonnay went on.

"I'd call him whatever he wanted me to call him, he's just *that* hot," China replied.

"Now, sugar," I began to advise, "this guy could be hot but she's givin' him some and he's been seen with her in public once?"

I left it at that but shook my head slowly.

"Daisy, serious," China said. "I was at that party. I saw him. And Bethany has talked about him. *A lot.* So even if half the shit she said is true, just getting a load of him, I'd not only call him whatever he wanted me to call him, I wouldn't care if we saw the light of day, just as long as he kept the lights on when he was doin' me. Because, I'll repeat, he's just *that hot.*"

"Well then," I murmured on a grin, "there you go."

There was a knock on the door and Wynter called out, "Decent."

Smithie swung in with the door, just his torso, his hand still on the knob, his scowl already set.

"Any a' you bitches feel like doin' somethin' other than sittin' around throwin' back a few beers, like, I don't know, *dancing?*"

"Is it time?" Chardonnay asked.

Smithie's gaze cut to the big clock on the wall that said yes, the day girls were done, the night girls were on seven minutes ago.

He didn't use those words. He just returned his scowl to the room.

The day girls didn't leave the stage until the night girls scooted out.

So it was definitely time for them to hit it.

"Right, we better go," Ashlynn said, setting her beer aside.

"Thanks for the cake. I can't wait to try some during your first set," Wynter added, shooting me a smile.

I gave her a smile back.

"Knock 'em dead, sugars!" I called after them.

Smithie didn't move, glowering at them as they filed out in front of him.

After China, the last of them, cleared the room, his eyes came to me.

"Sloan's booth is empty and the place is already packed. I need the space if he ain't gonna show. He comin' tonight?"

I nodded, feeling my heart squeeze and not in a good way.

I'd been back at work for over five weeks.

If I was working, most nights, at some point during the night, Marcus slid into the semi-circular booth at the very end on the north side of the club. A booth that had become his. No one sat at it because, first, it was Marcus Sloan's and second, Smithie put a red velvet rope in front of it until he showed.

Sometimes I'd watch from the dancers' hall, and when I did, I'd see that he didn't watch the dancers (though I noticed his eyes never left me when I was onstage). He would either be on his phone, talking to one of his men, or going over papers he had on the table while he sipped his bourbon and branch.

Whether Marcus showed or not, Brady stood outside the dressing room door if I was in it. If I was onstage, he stood just offstage, eyes on the club.

Yes, Marcus gave me his bodyguard.

After the night was done, if Marcus was there, Brady escorted me out the back door and into Marcus's limo. If he wasn't, Brady escorted me to my Porsche then followed me wherever I went after and then escorted me behind closed doors once I got there.

That *there* usually being Marcus's place, sometimes my place, though that was rarely.

If I had a day off and it wasn't a weekend (and I was a headliner and weekends were big for Smithie's, so it was rare I had time off on the weekends), I'd do my thing, Marcus would do his, but we'd meet for dinner.

The majority of the time he took me to fancy places. The other times, I made him let me cook for him (yes, I'd horned in on his kitchen). Twice, he got takeout but it wasn't from Twin Dragon or alternate goodness like that. It was always from swanky places that didn't even do takeout (except for men like Marcus).

In the beginning, I slept in his big bed, him in his guest room, or the times we were at my place, he insisted on sleeping on the couch.

Giving me hope, about two weeks ago, I got him to messing around in his bed, and even though he stopped the good stuff, he didn't leave. He got on his pajama bottoms (silk, drawstring, navy-blue, f-i-n-e, *fine*) and joined me there.

And from then on, we slept together.

Without, it was important to add, *sleeping together*.

He held me when we slept. Or he didn't move all night if I cuddled up to him.

That was good.

But I will repeat, we slept together without *sleeping together*.

That was bad.

He'd slid into second base repeatedly. And he was good at that in a big way. And once (giving me more hope), with his fingers over my panties, he'd given me the *very* good stuff.

But only once and that was it.

Mostly, he stopped the festivities before they got too heated, turned me into his arms or let me snuggle into him, gave me a soft kiss on my nose or forehead, and then we went to sleep.

And I'll repeat something else.

That was *it*.

For *over five weeks*.

We'd had conversations about this. Twelve of them to be exact. (Yes, I was counting.)

And I was getting nowhere except to know *really* well Marcus thought we should "take it slow."

I hadn't had a drama since my first time eating at his dining room table. I'd never had another nightmare. Not to mention, he knew I was no fragile flower. And I was giving him every indication I was ready to move us forward.

I understood why he wanted to take it slow and that was sweet.

But this wasn't slow.

This was alarming.

Because, see, shit like this messed with a girl's head.

A man doesn't want down her pants, that speaks volumes.

Or, more to the point, it makes a girl ask a lot of questions that might not seem logical to some, but to a girl, they were as logical as it could get.

For me, these questions were two in particular.

The first, was I the damsel in distress in place of the sister he'd wished he could save? And part B of that question, was he in denial about that, thinking he was doing the right thing when he was *not?*

Or second, was I a kind of employee he was looking after to keep safe while they kept looking for the guy who did what he'd done to me?

And no one had said anything, so I reckoned he was still out there. Detective Jimmy Marker had called at least ten times to share that he was disappointed with the progress of the case, but he had no intention of giving up so they were still looking.

Sure, the illogical part in all of this was that it had been way more than five weeks where Marcus had been sweet to me, kind, thoughtful, attentive, gentlemanly, generous, and even sexy. That should speak volumes too.

But, I mean, in my life, one of the many things I'd learned was that if a guy wants it, it's offered, he takes it. Especially if it's offered *repeatedly.*

So Marcus not taking it had to mean he didn't want it.

Now he'd seen me doing my thing on the stage and he'd seen it a lot. He was sweet as usual when I got in his limo with him after work. Complimentary. Touchy. Kissy. Nice. He hadn't acted, not once, like watching me do my gig made him think I was skeevy. Not even close.

In fact, it was the opposite.

It could not be said when he first started coming to the club it didn't make me feel all kinds of special, not only that he'd come, but that his eyes never left me when I was onstage, like he was transfixed, spellbound.

And not just in the beginning, that kept right on going, in actions and words, he gave me the sense he was proud of me. Proud that, at the end of the night, the woman he was watching onstage was going to be escorted to his limousine and she'd be spending the night in his bed (even if they didn't do much there).

But he was total class. He had a penthouse. He belonged to a country club (one he had not taken me to, by the way). He worked a lot and said things into his phone like "dividends" and "shift those investments around" and "the rate of return on that is not what I'd hoped, let's consider alternatives."

And I was, well, a stripper.

I had a Porsche but I didn't have a limo or a penthouse, and even though I raked it in (with him paying me, but I could have done it my own damned self if he hadn't taken off a set, a song on each set, and the lap dances), I'd never have that. I'd never belong to a country club. I'd never tame my hair, ease up on the eyeliner, and trade my platforms for Valentino's Rockstud in order to fit in with that set.

So maybe in the throes of the situation he'd gotten himself into a spot—being a gentleman and being the kind of gentleman Marcus Sloan was—a spot he couldn't get out of, dumping the chick who'd recently been raped after realizing she didn't quite fit at his side.

I didn't need that shit.

I needed to start looking for houses, dining room tables, and checking out china patterns.

And I didn't need to do it with a broken heart (though, I wasn't letting myself go there, but I had a strong feeling that ship had sailed).

Because even without the *good stuff*, everything else was good stuff with Marcus Sloan. And I was not talking about the fancy restaurants, the penthouse, the limo.

I was talking about his sweet. His attention that, even the times he was on the phone, he still made it clear if I was in his sphere, it was always on me. His touchy. His kissy. His arms around me while I slept. His warm, hard body the perfection it was to cuddle into. The easy way that came often that I could make him laugh. The beautiful way he looked at me every time he gave me the same.

So I'd let my heart get in it. He'd put that effort in but everyone had to take responsibility for their lives and I'd *let* him in when I knew I shouldn't. I knew he was too good for me. I knew it just wasn't my lot to get my something special.

And although most of his behavior indicated he wanted to be in, there was that one important way it did not. The intimacy we would share to make all the rest of it concrete in my head. To understand irrevocably that he wanted *all* of me. Not to save me. Not to take care of me. Not to go that extra mile because he was the man he was to look after an employee, or just some woman that occupied a fringe of his life, who had the worst done to her that could happen.

No, not any of that.

To have *me*.

Daisy.

"Woman?"

I focused on Smithie to see he was very focused on me.

"You good?" he asked.

I nodded, throwing him a dazzling smile.

He wasn't dazzled.

His eyes narrowed.

"Everything good with Sloan?" he pressed.

"Peachy," I lied.

It was good. It was just that *everything* wasn't good.

"You need me, I'm here," he stated and my heart that had started to go cold again warmed up a bit. "And if you gotta talk about guy stuff, LaTeesha is there."

I giggled a little bit and that made some of the concern drift out of Smithie's face.

"I need you or LaTeesha, I know where to find you," I told him.

He jerked up his chin.

Then he swung out.

I took another sip of my beer.

Then I turned to the mirror and picked up my teasing comb.

I was on in less than an hour. I needed to get ready.

* * * *

I slid down the pole upright, only one arm and one leg wrapped around it. My other arm was thrown out, my other leg extended up, my back arched, my head hanging back, my hair dangling.

When I got close to the bottom, I arched back further, put one hand then the other to the stage, did a layout but ended it dropping and tucking into a backward, one and a half somersault.

I ended that on my back, my hips twisted to the side, knees bent, legs tucked tight.

I straightened my legs and swung them wide, up and over, letting them take my body with them until I was on my forearms and knees.

I stuck my booty toward the end of the stage and felt the bills stuffed into my strings.

I was singing with the song that was playing—Lil' Kim, Christina Aguilera, Pink, and Mya's version of "Lady Marmalade"—but I stopped just to give one of the men who'd tipped me an air kiss before I popped up, legs straight and wide, head hanging down between them.

I slapped my hands to the stage and lifted up, throwing my hair back in a dramatic toss, turning and strutting down the stage in time to the song, swaying my hips.

I made the end, turned, and swung my ass out, feeling the cash flutter at my feet. I stuck the tip of my finger between my glossed lips, looked over my shoulder, gave a wink to no one, then ran back up the stage.

I launched myself at a pole, swung around it with body out, legs wide, through the ending of the song, finishing it on the floor in a front split, bent over, bared tits pressed toward the stage, head thrown back, mouth open.

Before the lights went black, I slid my eyes sideways.

Beyond the men standing up and cheering, I saw Marcus sitting in his booth, eyes on me, forearm on the table, fingers wrapped around his forgotten bourbon.

His lips were curved up in a smile that through the dark, even when my heart was breaking, I felt in my coochie.

He disappeared as the lights went out.

The crowd shouted but I pushed up and quickly exited the stage.

Holding out my robe for me, Brady gave me the grin that he always gave me when I left the stage, not leering and creepy, just appreciative.

Once he helped me on with my robe, he followed me, close to my back, to the dressing room as the girls rushed by, Chardonnay and China giving me high fives as they went.

I hit the dressing room door and turned back to Brady.

"I'll be out in about fifteen, sugar."

"All right, Daisy."

He opened the door for me, swept the room with his eyes, and closed the door after I went in.

I stood staring at the door, breathing heavy, and not just from the dance.

My eyes felt weirdly too dry.

And I was wondering how I was going to do what I needed to do next.

That was, get to Marcus's place.

And then let him off the hook.

In other words…

I was going to break up with him.

* * * *

In my ice-blue Juicy Couture tracksuit with its decal on the back of the hoodie that had peach and blue hibiscus flowers around a gold, interlaced "JC," the same flowers on the front hip of the pants, I slid out of the cold Denver air into the warmth of the limo beside Marcus.

I did this grinning up at Brady.

"Thanks, darlin'."

He grinned back. "Not a problem, Daisy."

He closed the door and I tried to look at Marcus, but I had to do it quickly looking *through* Marcus.

What I saw was that he was still in his suit, like he was always still in his suit when he came to see me dance, except on the weekends. This telling me he didn't waste time going home to change.

He came right to me.

I wished I could believe the reasons behind what that seemed to mean were real.

"Hey," I greeted him quickly, then looked to the front, into the sunglassed eyes I saw in the rearview mirror. "Hey, Ronald."

"Yo," he grunted.

That was usually the most I got out of Ronald and that was all I got out of him then as he started us moving along the back of Smithie's.

I kept my eyes there, thanking the Lord my Porsche was in the parking spot closest to the elevators in Marcus's garage (a spot Marcus insisted I parked in the minute he gave me the remote to his garage). That would make it (slightly) easier to get away once I did what I had to do.

This was my thought until the side of Marcus's forefinger and his thumb took gentle hold of my chin and he turned my head to face him.

"Hey," he said softly.

"Hey," I repeated my earlier greeting.

"Everything okay?"

I gave him the lie I gave Smithie. He'd learn it was a lie in about fifteen minutes, but whatever.

I'd get this done.

And I was Daisy.

So no matter how much it tore me apart, I'd then move on.

Which meant Marcus would be able to move on to a woman that suited him.

That woman obviously not being me.

That lie was, "Peachy."

He didn't let my chin go, and in the streetlights that illuminated the interior of the car, he studied me.

"You sure?" he asked.

God, I hated that he could read me.

I nodded, still held in his light grip. "Yep."

It took him another couple of moments to let me go. When he did, I looked to my knees.

"You were great tonight," he stated.

"Thanks, sugar," I muttered.

"You're always great."

"Thanks," I repeated.

"Party go okay?"

"Yeah."

"Your friend like her cake?"

I looked out the windshield and nodded.

"Good," Marcus murmured, sounding distracted.

I drew in a breath.

I let it go.

Marcus fell silent.

I did not fill that void.

Ronald drove us to Marcus's penthouse and he rode up with us and stood in the vestibule as Marcus let us in.

"Thank you, Ronald," Marcus said to him as I scooted in the door Marcus pushed open for me.

Ronald had no reply.

I looked out the windows at the lights of the city, the shadowed grandeur of the Front Range, hating it that was the last time I'd see that view and wishing in that moment something that gorgeous had never been given to me.

Wishing that so I wouldn't wish the same about other, more important things.

I heard the door close behind me.

I turned to Marcus.

"Ready for bed?" he asked.

"I'm leaving," I blurted.

That wasn't how I'd wanted to start it.

Then again, that was as good a way to start as any.

His body in the subdued lighting of elegant sconces glowing low on their dimmers visibly tightened.

"I'm sorry?" he asked quietly.

"I'm leaving," I repeated.

"You're…leaving," he said slowly.

"I…uh, yeah."

"Why?"

I didn't answer that.

I said, "It'd be nice if you texted me a time when I could come back and get my stuff and arrange for someone to let me into your penthouse."

The air in the room changed.

I ignored it.

"Why?" he repeated, sounding more terse, in other words, demanding.

"I just really need to go. Now," I told him.

"Without telling me why?" he pushed.

I knew it wasn't fair. It wasn't right.

But I guessed I didn't have in me what I needed to have in me to do this fair and right.

Not even for Marcus.

Because I was leaving Marcus.

"Can we just please make this easy?" I requested.

"You wish to come back and get your stuff. This indicates you're leaving and not coming back. Except to collect your things."

"Yes," I whispered.

"Why?"

I swallowed.

"Did something happen?" he asked.

I shook my head.

"Then why?"

"Marcus, please."

"Tell me…"

And then I jumped when he completely lost it and I'd never seen Marcus lose it, not ever, and definitely not with me.

He did this leaning toward me and shouting, "*Why?*"

"You don't want me," I returned.

His torso reared back.

"Are you insane?" he asked.

"You won't sleep with me," I replied.

"I've been sleeping with you for weeks."

"Right," I bit out, losing it myself. "I'll say it different. You won't fuck me."

"No, Daisy, I'll never fuck you."

My head jerked like he'd slapped me.

"I'll never fuck you," he repeated and went on, "You aren't that woman to me."

"Right." It came out weak, broken, pained. "So, now can I leave?"

"Christ, you don't get it," he clipped.

"You're right," I returned. "I'm not *gettin' it*."

"Daisy, we need to take this slow," he informed me, sounding like he was seeking patience.

"And that's been your excuse since the beginning," I shot back.

His voice was low and dangerous when he asked, "Excuse?"

"A man wants a piece of ass, it's on offer, he has it, and it's been on offer, Marcus, *for weeks*. So, you see, you not takin' it tells me you don't want it."

"You *are* insane," he said softly, like he wasn't even talking to me.

"No. I'm not. I'm a woman falling in love with a man who doesn't want me."

I watched his body jerk in surprise.

"Daisy—"

Honestly?

I could take no more.

And who could fucking, *fucking* blame me?

"Fuck this!" I exploded, the emotion coursing through me taking control so I couldn't stop myself lifting my hands in fists over my head and shaking them. I dropped them and shouted, "Just let me fucking *leave!*"

"You called me, terrified."

Hunh?

"What?" I asked.

"That night. That night you called me and you were terrified. I've never seen anything like the state of you when I got to you. I arrived in your room, Daisy, you were curled into a corner, awake, but lost in a nightmare. Did you even know I was there?"

"Of course I knew," I snapped.

"Do you know what you said to me?"

That I didn't remember, seeing as he was right. I was lost in a nightmare. Though I was worried I'd babbled on about building my castles.

To cover that, I hissed, "I know you were there."

"Right," he whispered, totally seeing through me. Then he declared, "He scraped your ass raw on that asphalt."

I winced and looked away.

Marcus kept at me.

"He did not fuck you. He did not bang you. He did not have sex with you. He *raped* you. Do you get the difference?"

"Yeah," I bit out sarcastically, turning back to him with squinty eyes, my face hard. "I was there, darlin'. I get it a fuckuva lot better than you."

"But he was inside you."

Oh God.

I started shaking.

"Stop talkin'," I demanded.

He did not stop talking.

Oh no.

He did not.

"And I'm the man who has to come after that. How do I do that, Daisy? How do I do that and make sure you don't go back there? How do I do that and make sure it's good for you? Make sure I take you where I want us to be? Give you that at the same time keeping you safe? Give you what I want you to get from me? Make you understand what being inside you means to me?"

I stood still, staring at him, frozen, but I did it still trembling.

Though now for a different reason.

"How, Daisy?" he pushed.

I kept staring, trembling, unable to speak.

Marcus was able to speak.

"I talked with a woman called Bex who's worked for years at a rape crisis center. She told me to be watchful, communicative, patient, and *give it time*. We need to *give it time* so I can be certain to give you what you deserve when I give you me."

"You don't wanna fuck me," I whispered.

"No, I don't want to fuck you," he bit off.

"You want to make love to me."

"Yes, that's what I want to do and that's what I need you to feel when I do it."

Oh my God.

I was in love with this man.

And he was in love with me.

He was in love with me.

"Marcus?"

"What?" he clipped.

"Please make love to me."

We stood staring at each other in the dim lights in his fabulous entryway.

But all of a sudden I had my hand in his and was being dragged up an elegant winding staircase.

I tripped.

Marcus stopped, jerked my arm, and then I was flying through the air.

I settled in his arms like a bride carried by her groom as he stalked up the rest of the steps and prowled down the hall to his room.

"Seriously, really, truly," I whispered to his hard jaw. "If you're carryin' me in this way to your bedroom, honey bunches of love, somethin' needs to come to fruition."

He looked down at me when he cleared the doorway then he walked me across his room and slid me down his body so I could take my feet when he made it to the side of the bed.

He bent to the side to switch on a light but straightened in front of me, right in my space.

"Are you leaving me?" he asked.

"Never," I answered.

That was when he kissed me.

We fell back to the bed when Marcus pressed into me.

I immediately went after his suit jacket.

He went after the zip of my hoodie.

He let me win and I shoved the jacket down his shoulders.

He threw it off and then took down the zip.

I yanked his shirt out of his trousers and dove in at the back.

God, not for the first time I encountered skin that felt *amazing*.

Through all this, Marcus kissed me.

Suddenly, he rolled so he was on his back, I was on top, and he sat up, so I was forced to straddle him.

My coochie liked the kissing.

It liked the straddling better.

"Baby," I whispered.

He pushed the hoodie down my shoulders.

I tossed it away.

His eyes holding mine, he went after the back clasp of my bra.

His fingers there, and that was it.

He needed me to give him permission. To let him know where I was at. To show him I was with him, only him, this was only him and me.

God.

Marcus Sloan.

"Please," I breathed.

It came loose then the bra was gone.

He looked at me exposed to him in his bed for the first time, not on a stage, and he whispered, "So beautiful."

God.

Marcus Sloan.

"Kiss me, honey," I begged.

His hands went up my back, into my hair, pulling my face to his, and he kissed me.

He did a lot of kissing. In fact, he kept my mouth occupied with his lips and tongue the whole time it took him to get my clothes off, his clothes off (but he let me help with that part). And he kissed me the whole time he touched me, no, *caressed me*, his hands roaming, slow, gentle, sweet, over every inch of me.

Finally, *finally*, he bent and took my nipple in his mouth.

That shot so hot up my coochie, I slid my fingers in his hair, my neck twisting to the side, and I gasped, "Yes."

He worked me there just like he always worked me with his kisses these past weeks and everything he'd done that night.

Slow. Gentle. Sweet.

And just the same way, as his lips moved to my other nipple, his hand slid over my hip, over my belly and down.

I opened my legs for him.

His fingers slid through me.

My lips parted, my hips lifted, his mouth went away, and I righted my head to catch his gaze.

Watching me, his face dark and beautiful, he stroked a finger inside.

And when he did, his face got darker, more beautiful.

And *hungry*.

My hands darted out and clutched his arms, my eyes drifting closed, I whimpered, "Marcus."

His thumb hit me, my body jolted, my eyes shot open, and I saw he was still watching me.

"Inside," I gasped.

"In a minute, baby."

"Inside," I pleaded.

"Daisy—"

I lifted my hands to wrap them around either side of his neck, moaned as his thumb put on more pressure, and then I demanded huskily, "I need you *inside*, honey."

He was Marcus.

He didn't make me ask again.

He rolled between my legs. I felt his hand leave me but right after something hard and silky started gliding, sliding.

And then...

Then...

Eyes locked to mine, slow, gentle, sweet, Marcus Sloan, my man, the man every step of my life had been leading me to, slid inside me.

"Now, this..." I breathed. "*This* is where I was always meant to be."

Beauty scored through his expression before his head dropped, he shoved his face in my neck and he groaned, "Daisy."

I turned so I had my mouth to his ear. "Take what's yours, baby."

He did.

Pulling his face out of my neck, taking my mouth, he moved inside me and he took what was his.

Giving himself to me.

And a whole lot more.

I cried the intensity of my orgasm down his throat, clutching him with everything I had, limbs wrapped around, fingers gripping his hair, body shuddering.

He returned the beauty when his head snapped back, he buried himself inside me, his body bucked into mine, and I received it gratefully (still shuddering).

When he was done, he dropped to me but only for a breath before he rolled us but kept us connected and held me tight on top of him.

My forehead pressed to the side of his neck, I didn't bother trying to steady my breathing. I just let each breath rush out against his skin as I committed every second of the last twenty minutes to memory.

Every *second*.

It was only when I felt his fingertips drawing patterns on my hip that I realized both our breaths were steady.

His fingers clenched into my flesh suddenly and his voice was thick and astounding when he asked, "You're falling in love with me?"

I drew in breath.

Then I lifted my head and looked down at him.

God, he wasn't handsome.

He was everything.

"I was," I answered.

His sated gaze went guarded.

"You were?"

"That ship has sailed, sugar. And I'm on it. It's called," I drawled out my last, "the *Love Boat.*"

And I grinned when, under me and all around, I heard, saw, and felt my man burst out laughing.

Chapter Ten

The Second
Marcus

When it was almost too late, Marcus pulled out of Daisy's mouth and got to his knees in their bed.

Her torso shot up so she was on her knees, too.

Her eyes also narrowed and she snapped, "I wasn't done!"

Marcus hooked her with his arm around her waist, felt her surprised, breathy cry carve through his throbbing cock as he lifted her up and swung her in front of him.

He turned them so her back was to the headboard.

One arm around her, his other hand guiding the way, he slid her down on him.

Her head fell back, her hair brushing his arm.

He fell forward, on top of her. Her platinum hair all over his pillows, he lifted an arm to brace his hand against the headboard and he started moving.

She focused with effort on him.

"You're done," he growled.

She gave him a dazed grin.

He kissed her.

Five minutes later, he made her come.

A minute after that, she gave him the same.

* * * *

It had been three days since they'd consummated their relationship.

Three days Marcus gave Daisy to get used to this change. Three days Marcus gave himself to watch over her and make sure she was good with the change.

And three days for him to get over being pissed she'd tried to leave him.

She was good with the change if the amount, variety, and magnificence of the sex was anything to go by.

He wasn't complaining. Weeks with her in his life and the last of those with her sweet little body, beautiful face, and all that gorgeous damned hair sleeping beside him in his bed had been torture. He was fucking thrilled it was over.

Obviously because the torture was over.

But mostly because Daisy was good with it.

However, to be certain, he'd called Bex and discussed the change with her.

"It's a process," she'd explained. "Some people adjust. Some people it takes longer. Some people let it haunt them. If you perceive this is going well, just keep doing what you've been doing. Be watchful. Encourage her to communicate. And be patient. She'll never be over this, Mr. Sloan. I think you understand this isn't a bruise that fades away. It's coming to the understanding that what happened, happened. It was no fault of hers. Then learning how to cope with the fact it happened and giving herself permission to move on. That's the key. But if you can show her you're a man who'll handle her with care, that you'll be there in those times she needs to cope, then I have every faith you two will be good."

One thing Marcus knew, Daisy could cope with anything.

The thing he didn't know was if she knew he would always be there to help.

So right then, after they'd shared what they'd shared on a night when she didn't have to work so they had all night to get through what he needed them to get through, he was going to make certain she knew that.

"We need to talk," he declared.

She stopped tracing patterns on his chest with a pearl-white fingernail that had a pink tip with a swirl of black across it, the black embedded with rhinestones.

She lifted her head from his shoulder and looked at him.

"Uh-oh," she mumbled the minute she did.

Marcus tightened his arm around her at his side and pulled her over his chest.

Then he clamped his other arm around her.

"I'm thinkin' this is a serious talk, you need me fixed to your chest," she kept mumbling, her eyes aimed at his chin.

"This is serious, darling, so please look at me while you listen to me."

She looked into his eyes.

She was holding her body stiffly and Marcus wanted to shake her.

She was preparing for the worst.

This shouldn't be a surprise, not with the life she'd led.

However, Daisy lost it with him taking his time completing them. The operative part of that was *taking his time*.

She was far from dumb.

And he'd taken his time and taught her better.

Holding his patience, he stated, "I handle you with care."

She stared at him.

"Have I ever not done that?" he asked.

"No," she said slowly.

"So you know that."

"Yes."

"So why are you tensed and looking freaked out?"

"Uh...I don't know, because you're freaking me out."

"How am I doing that?"

"You're bein' real serious and we just had a fun time, sugar. After fun times don't come serious times. After fun times there's cuddling and whispers which lead to kissing and groping and then more fun times. Unless you're sleepy, then they lead to sleepy times. They don't lead to serious times."

A variety of things with Daisy would be a lot easier if she wasn't so goddamned cute.

"You don't use your last name," he announced.

She stared at him again.

"Smithie's got it on your employment records but you don't use it. Ever. None of the girls know it. None of the bouncers. Waitresses. Nobody."

"Well, I'm Daisy like Cher's Cher and Charo is Charo. But I'm more like Charo. She has better hair…and cleavage."

Yes, a variety of things would be easier if Daisy wasn't so fucking cute.

"That's not it," he pushed.

Haltingly, she replied, "I…it's not mine. It's…well, *his*. And he hasn't been a part of me in, uh…maybe really in forever."

"You're right. It's not yours. You're Daisy. And the only last name you'll ever really have is Sloan."

Her body lurched on top of him.

He just held her tighter.

"So let's get this straight, shall we?" he suggested.

"Okay," she whispered, her eyes bright and still staring.

Marcus had a feeling with what he'd already said she had it straight.

But he went about making certain.

"I handle you with care. I'll *always* handle you with care. I will never, not ever, Daisy, give you reason to leave me. I won't cheat on you. I won't beat you. The gambles I take will be in business only, but you'll always be covered financially regardless. I like to drink but I never drink too much. I've never taken drugs in my life. I like control and you can't be in control inebriated or stoned. To end, you're safe with me. You'll get from me only what you deserve, which is everything I can give you doing it handling you with care."

"Okay, sugar." She was still whispering.

"Is that completely understood?"

She nodded.

She was staring at him so closely he decided she did understand.

Completely.

Regardless, he kept going.

"If I break any of those promises, you're free to leave me. If I don't, you're not. Not ever. If something isn't working, we talk it out and make it work. Which means we'll always work so there will be no reason to leave."

With that, a different understanding was all over her face when she said softly, "I got stuff twisted in my head, Marcus."

"That was clear."

"It's untwisted now, baby."

"Good."

She drew her fingers down his jaw, dropping her face closer to his.

"Never gonna leave you, Marcus."

"Good," he grunted.

"God," she whispered, her gaze moving over his face. "Who woulda thought, givin' my heart, havin' it broken, learnin' to guard it, I'd learn something else one day. That bein' the best way to keep it safe is to find a man who'd prove he could handle it with care and give it to him."

That felt good.

Fucking good.

So fucking good, he'd never felt anything that good in his whole goddamned life.

But Marcus didn't share that with her because he knew without a single doubt she knew it too.

"I'm glad you got that part, Daisy. It's important."

She looked into his eyes.

"Now," he continued, rolling them to their sides, "we can get to the cuddling, whispering, and groping part."

She smiled at him, a brilliant flash of teeth added to a dazzling flash of humor in her cornflower-blue eyes.

Then she started giggling, filling their bedroom with the sound of bells.

While doing that, she kissed him.

This meant they skipped the cuddling and whispering parts and got right into groping.

And again, Marcus wasn't complaining.

* * * *

His phone rang.

Marcus rolled.

Daisy rolled with him.

She snuggled into his back as he looked at the display.

At what he saw, he kept his body loose as he flipped his phone open.

"Yes?"

"Lee got him. We're at the warehouse," Darius said.

Nightingale got him.

Finally.

"I'll be there in twenty," he told Darius.

"Right," Darius replied.

He felt Daisy press into his back.

Marcus flipped his phone shut and turned to her.

"Everything okay?" she asked sleepily, but he heard the concern in her voice.

"Everything's fine. I just need to go see to something."

She'd clearly looked at his bedside clock because she asked, "At three in the morning?"

"Yes."

She got up on a forearm. "Does this happen a lot?"

"No."

They fell silent as he slid a hand up her hip to her back and moved into her.

"Right. Okay. You're comin' right back?" she asked.

He grinned.

Fuck, his Daisy.

"Yes," he said against her mouth.

She let him take it for a brief, deep kiss then she didn't let him go, brushing soft, light kisses on his lips before she finally stopped.

"Be safe," she whispered.

"I will, darling. And I won't be long."

He watched her hair nod in the dark.

He kissed her nose.

Then he rolled out of bed and made sure the covers were over her before he moved to his walk-in closet.

He called Ronald from there and spoke to him quietly.

That done, he dressed.

* * * *

Marcus walked into the warehouse, Brady at his back, Louie at his, Vince at his. Ronald was standing outside by the car.

The space was large. There was a couch in it, a folding table with two chairs, a deck of cards on it arrested in a game. Hiding a corner, there was some ripped, opaque-with-grime plastic sheeting hanging from the ceiling, a good deal of dust on the floor, and not much else.

However, the room was populated.

Darius Tucker was there, standing next to his aunt, Shirleen Jackson.

Darius was a tall, lean black man with twists in his hair and a face that would be handsome if it wasn't so cold.

Shirleen was a tall, full-figured black woman with a very large Afro. She was wearing purple and looked like she'd come to that warehouse from choir practice at a church where all the women vied to be best dressed.

Standing opposite them, there was a man built like a linebacker. His dark hair was thick and wavy, his dark-brown eyes were alert and locked on Marcus. He was wearing jeans, brown boots, and a long-sleeved cargo shirt.

Lee Nightingale.

At his side was a man known on the streets as Stark. His last name. His first was Lucas but everyone called him Stark, unless you were someone he'd allow to call him Luke, and there weren't many of those. He had black hair, dark-blue eyes, a full beard that was trimmed precisely along his jaw, and he was wearing black cargo pants, a tight, black, wicking shirt, and black combat boots.

And last, there was a man on his knees. His hands were not bound. But his head was bent forward and it looked like he was listing.

Shirleen and Darius had been playing.

Perhaps Nightingale and Stark, too.

Though, at a glance, Marcus noted it was only Stark who had cut, bloody knuckles.

Marcus stopped and looked behind him.

Brady jerked up his chin but it was Louie who moved forward.

He went to the man on his knees, grasped him by his hair, and yanked his head back.

The man grunted but nothing else. However, he looked like he'd keel over if Louie didn't keep hold of him.

Although his face was blooded and very swollen, there was no mistaking he was the man Marcus saw in the video in Smithie's security room.

The man who'd raped Daisy.

He nodded to Louie, who let him go.

He swayed so Marcus ordered, "Make him keep his knees."

Louie dropped his eyes to the man.

Marcus looked to Shirleen but he said nothing.

"Figure that's my invitation to take my leave," she muttered, shot him a grin, and said louder, "Time's right, Marcus, Shirleen'll be wantin' to meet your girl."

Shirleen was a resourceful businesswoman.

She was also loyal as they came.

"I'll be certain that's arranged."

Her grin got wide and white, then she looked to Darius.

Eyes to his aunt, he tipped his head to the door.

She nodded to him, looked through everyone in the room, except the man on the floor she walked right up to.

"Aunt Shirleen," Darius growled in a low, warning tone.

"You're a pig," she whispered down at the man on his knees.

His head swung not entirely in his control to the side in order to look away.

Shirleen stood in contemplation over him for several long moments before she turned and walked from the room, her high heels sounding loud in the open space.

When that sound disappeared, Marcus looked to Nightingale.

"Darius tells me this was you."

Nightingale tilted up his chin. "Got a new tracker. He's good. So far, no one's been able to hide from him. When we were getting nothing in Denver, we set him on it. He found this guy in Montana. Persuaded him to share his story. That being, Smithie gave Jimmy Marker the guy's name from credit card receipts. Marker rolled up to his house with some squads, so he knew your woman pressed charges. He was twitchy, not sure how she'd play it, so he was also on the lookout. Before the boys could get into position, he took off out the back. He waited until the coast was clear, got as much together as he could, and left town."

Marcus gave him a nod and looked to Stark but said to Nightingale, "In future business, you don't need a second."

"Luke's here because he helped Vance do the persuading and he's feelin' the need to see this through," Nightingale responded.

That explained the bloody knuckles.

"Your tracker?" Marcus asked, eyes still on Stark.

"Vance needs clear of certain things," Nightingale answered.

This meant his tracker was an ex-con.

It was good to know Nightingale was protective. It said a great deal. It was also good to know Nightingale hired with a view to the future, not judging what was in the past. That said more.

Marcus spoke directly to Stark. "You shouldn't be here."

Stark was known not to be a big talker. This he proved by not replying but also not moving.

"You don't want to be here," Marcus warned.

Stark spoke again without speaking, doing this crossing his arms on his chest.

Marcus looked to Nightingale. "You should take your man and go."

"I'm feelin' the need to see this through, too."

Marcus held his gaze. "Detective Marker is not going to close this case."

Nightingale did nothing but put his hands on his hips.

"Your father is a cop, your brother is a cop, and your best friend is a cop," Marcus pointed out.

"Yeah, and none of them are here," Nightingale returned.

"You're also not going to dissuade me," Marcus shared.

"Am I doing any dissuading?" Nightingale asked.

Marcus studied him.

Then he told him quietly, "I'm protecting you."

A flash shot through Nightingale's eyes.

Rage.

"I saw that fuckin' tape," he bit out. "And just sayin', so did Vance and so did Luke. So I think you more than anybody get me when I say Luke and me feel the need to see this through."

He was young.

He was good at what he did, but he was young.

He'd learn.

Rage had no place in what they did, Nightingale's place skirting the edges of it, Marcus's right in the middle of it.

You gave in to your rage, you got sloppy.

In their game, sloppy men didn't survive.

You planned.

You executed.

Then you moved on.

"Let me protect you," Marcus urged.

They locked eyes and it took some time but eventually Nightingale proved he wasn't only good, he was smart. He did this jerking up his chin, cutting his gaze through Stark, and he dropped his hands from his hips before he cast a glance at Tucker and strode away.

Stark stared at Marcus another beat before he dropped his arms from his chest and followed Nightingale.

Marcus waited until the sound of the heavy door closing echoed through the room and only then did he look at Darius.

"It's arranged?" he asked.

"Zano and Townsend are both on board." Darius walked to Marcus, pulling a gun out of the back of his jeans and offering it Marcus's way.

Marcus took it.

Darius continued, "They find anything, it'll be linked to the House of Shade. Everyone wants Shade out. He's sliding, somethin' surfaces with this, things'll get a lot more slippery."

"Is something going to surface?" Marcus asked.

Darius shrugged. Then he smiled.

Christ.

Cold as stone.

A long time ago, Shirleen's now-dead husband made things very difficult for Vincent Shade. He was holding on mostly because there was always enough crime to go around, and even stupid and completely insane, Shade managed to find his share.

He'd been a nuisance for some time.

Darius was correct, everyone wanted him gone. It was just that, considering he was only a nuisance, no one felt any need to expend much effort to see to that task.

Marcus could not know if Shirleen and Darius had reason to lose patience and intended to deal a killing blow.

And he didn't care.

He looked to the man on his knees.

"Vincetti's clean up," Darius muttered and Marcus knew he was on the move. "Dom and his boys're en route. Ren is not in the know on this and Vito wants it kept that way."

"Thank you," Marcus replied.

"Serious, this piece of shit, don't mention it," Darius said as his farewell.

Marcus waited again until he heard the door close.

Then he focused on the man's eyes.

He was looking up at Marcus.

"Why?" Marcus asked.

"Just finish it," the guy mumbled.

"Why?" Marcus repeated.

"*Fuck!*" the man exploded, the force of it making him veer forward so he had to put a hand out to catch his fall. He didn't right himself but tipped his head back and shouted, "*Just finish it!*"

Louie pulled him back up to his knees by his hair.

"*Fucking finish it!*" he screamed, ripping his head from Louie's hold, listing again but keeping his knees.

"Why?" Marcus asked again.

"We gonna play this game?" the man asked snidely.

"I'm thinking you might not have absorbed this, but this is my game, so yes, we're going to play it."

The man glared at him then spat, "Had me ejected."

"It's my understanding you put your hands on her during a private dance. That's not allowed at Smithie's."

"She's a fuckin' stripper," he hissed.

Marcus ignored that and he could because he'd learned early how to control his rage.

"You broke the rules, she had you ejected, so you raped her?"

"I know she's yours. I've heard your name. Didn't know it at the time but I sure as fuck know it now. I also know nothin' I say is gonna stop what you're gonna do. Maybe just make it last longer and be less fun, and serious, man, that guy with a beard and his Indian friend weren't a barrel of laughs. So not that I'm invitin' that shit, but just sayin', to top the joyride I had with those fuckin' guys, you'd have to get creative. But how about we skip this bullshit and you just fucking *finish it?*"

Interesting.

Shirleen and Darius hadn't played with him at all.

Only Stark and Nightingale's tracker.

This meant Nightingale and his team had no qualms with a variety of aspects of their business.

Marcus set these thoughts aside, studied the man before him for some time, and then whispered, "You can't answer me."

The man looked away and Louie used his hair to make him look back.

"Fuck," he bit out.

"Do you have a mother?" Marcus asked.

"Fuck you," the man spat.

"Sisters?"

"Fuck...*you!*" he leaned forward and shouted.

Louie pulled him back.

"You do, so why?" Marcus pressed.

"Because I could, all right?" he yelled. "Because I fuckin' could and she couldn't fuckin' stop me that time, could she?"

Marcus tilted his head to the side. "That's it? Because you could?"

"Yeah, because I *could.*"

"So you're telling me you thought she bested you and your dick is so small, you couldn't bear that blow so you needed to show her who had the power?"

"Why do you do all the shit you do to wear your fancy suit and have your men at your back?" the man countered. "Don't stand there thinkin' you're better than me when you got me on my knees and you got a gun in your hand I know you're gonna use. Because for that reason right there, you aren't better than me, asshole."

"That's an interesting, but erroneous, comparison."

"Whatever," the guy muttered.

"I've never raped a woman."

"Oh, good. You're a saint," he bit back.

"I've never ordered a woman to be raped."

"Whatever, motherfucker, just *end this.*"

"The games I play, every player knows the score."

"Jesus, put you in a suit, you're a superhero."

"The point I'm trying to make is, she was an innocent woman walking through a parking lot not having any idea someone was going to commit a violent act using her body to do it. And what I'm trying to understand is how you could be that someone who'd commit that violent act using an innocent woman to do it."

"I mighta got my bell rung pretty fuckin' good by those two fuckin' assholes, but I'm not missin' your point."

Simply out of curiosity, Marcus asked, "Have you done this before?"

"Never taken it all the way." He suddenly sneered at Marcus, showing him a set of bloody teeth, of which three were missing in a way Marcus knew they'd only been recently lost. "Your girl was my first." The sneer faded and a different kind of ugliness replaced it as he shook his head. "But no bitch disrespects me. *No bitch.* I had my way of communicatin' that, and I don't give a fuck I'm on my knees, I got no regrets. A bitch has it comin', that's just the way. You're too weak to get that, not my problem."

At that, Marcus heard from behind him Brady pull in a hiss of breath through his teeth.

This was not because the man on his knees had insulted Marcus.

Or, not entirely.

It was because Brady had three younger sisters and two shit-for-brains parents that got their asses incarcerated, one three weeks after the other, leaving an eighteen-at-the-time Brady the only one who could look after those girls like Marcus's sister had done, or let them hit the system.

He'd decided to look after his sisters.

Fortunately, he'd found Marcus not long after and Marcus helped him do that.

Nevertheless, for obvious reasons, Brady, like Marcus, wasn't a big fan of any man thinking it's just the way if "a bitch has it comin'."

Down low, Marcus swung a hand slightly out and he felt the heat of Brady's anger at his back subside.

He'd taught Brady the lesson about rage too.

Marcus focused again on the man.

"She was going to get her lip gloss."

"Do I care?"

"Her laugh sounds like bells."

"Again, asswipe, *do I care?*"

Again, Marcus studied him and he did it for a good length of time.

Closely.

"No," Marcus finally said, speaking quietly. "You don't. You don't care. And that's it. That's why you could do what you did. Because you don't care. I was right. You're nothing but an animal."

"You think I'm gonna beg for mercy, I'm not, fuckwad. Again, don't give a fuck she's convinced you different. That gash don't matter. Most gash don't matter. But her? *She's a fucking stripper!*"

The gunshot echoed loud through the room.

The man slumped to his back.

Marcus turned, Brady came to his side, and Marcus handed him the gun.

"You'll coordinate things with Dom?" he asked.

Brady nodded.

Marcus took that in.

Then he walked out of the warehouse.

* * * *

Sitting in the back of his car, Ronald driving, the phone held to his ear, Marcus heard it ring three times before Smithie answered with, "It's after four in the fuckin' morning."

"It's done."

There was silence then, "What's done?"

"Daisy's safe."

More silence before a muttered, "That Nightingale guy."

Marcus said nothing.

"This does not make me happy," Smithie announced.

Marcus felt his neck get tight. "How can this not make you happy?"

"'Cause, brother, whatever got done got done without me gettin' my licks in."

Marcus let out a breath. "You're not that man."

"Maybe you don't know me too good."

"I know you, Smithie, and you're not that man. But I am."

"Fuck," Smithie bit out, his way of conceding the point.

"She's safe. It's done. We can all move on."

Abruptly, Smithie asked, "You love her?"

Without hesitation, Marcus answered, "Yes."

Smithie was back to muttering. "Fuck, now I gotta find a new dancer."

Marcus smiled into the dark. "She likes to dance, Smithie, but yes. Eventually, she'll be busy having our children, and my guess is Daisy will feel the need to put all her attention into that."

"I like you enough to hope you don't have girls," Smithie mumbled.

Marcus hoped he did.

"Thank you for being the first man in her life she could trust," Marcus said.

Again, there was silence.

After Marcus gave him time for that, Smithie replied, "Thank you for bein' the second."

Then Smithie hung up.

Marcus flipped his phone shut and turned his head to look out the window in order to watch Denver slide by on his way home to Daisy.

* * * *

"Boss," Ronald growled.

Marcus stared out the windshield at Lee Nightingale standing beside the elevator doors, arms crossed on his chest, one booted foot up, the sole resting against the concrete.

Yes, Nightingale was good.

Marcus's building was secure. In other words, it had armed security guards that looked after everyone, not just Marcus. There were codes. There were monitored cameras. And Nightingale looked like he'd been waiting for some time, undisturbed.

"It's okay," Marcus said.

Ronald swung into his spot and bit out, "Fuck!" as Marcus threw open his own door.

Lee pushed away from the wall. Marcus closed his door and met him halfway across the short space.

Nightingale shoved his hand in his pocket as Ronald warned, "Not another move."

"It's fine, Ronald," Marcus said, not looking from Nightingale.

He pulled his hand out of his pocket, lifted it, and from his fingers dropped a necklace—delicate gold chain, at the bottom a row of pearls.

"Wasn't the time to give you this an hour ago," Nightingale muttered.

Marcus lifted his hand palm up.

Nightingale let the pearls go and they fell into his hand.

His fingers closed around it.

"Do you work on retainer?" Marcus asked.

Lee Nightingale's head twitched.

And then he smiled.

* * * *

Marcus slid into bed beside Daisy, gliding a hand over the silk at her belly and pulling her back into his front.

He curled into her.

Her fingers curled to link through his at her middle.

"Everything good?" she asked sleepily.

He buried his face in her hair.

"Everything is perfect."

Her fingers tensed in his.

He pulled her deeper into his body and whispered, "You're safe now, darling."

At that, her entire body tensed.

She let his hand go, turned in his arm, and slid hers around him.

He could feel her gaze in the dark.

"Are you okay?"

Marcus tangled his legs with hers.

"I'm fine, honey." He gave her a squeeze. "Are you?"

"Peachy."

He grinned.

She snuggled closer.

"Love you, baby," she whispered.

"Love you too, darling."

She stiffened then melted in his arms.

He'd had to wait to say it. He'd had to wait until he knew he'd done all he could to make it as right as he could make it.

He'd done that.

So he said it.

"A dream," she murmured.

"Sorry?"

"You. You're the dream a girl like me never thought she could dream."

She was right. She'd told him she'd never given herself a prince charming.

But now she had one in the way he came.

So all that was left was to build her a castle.

And Marcus was going to take care of that too.

Epilogue

Annamae
Daisy

I stood in the suite and stared out the windows at the snow-covered mountains while Michelle closed the door behind the girls who'd done my hair and makeup.

"Gosh, but you're the most beautiful thing I've ever seen."

I turned to watch Marcus's sister walking toward me and smiled. "Well, thanks, sugar."

She looked me up and down and then she got misty.

I moved to her, my skirt swaying with me, and it had to be said, it felt *nice*. So nice, I never wanted to take that dress off. Not ever.

But if I didn't, it wouldn't stay as pretty as it was.

And it'd be difficult for Marcus to give me some wedding nookie. He could get creative. But I didn't want any of his creative ruining my dress.

I got close and took her hands in mine.

"You gotta quit cryin', darlin'," I advised, doing so because she'd burst into tears no less than six times since she and Doug had met us up in Aspen two days before. "You got your makeup done too and you're pretty as a picture. Marcus and Doug'll be all upset you show puffy-eyed and red in the face."

"Marcus won't even know I'm there."

He loved his sister but I reckoned she had *that* right.

She pulled a hand from mine, lifted it, and cupped my jaw. "I'm glad he waited to find the right girl."

In response, I gave her the understatement of the century.

"I'm glad I *was* the right girl."

We grinned at each other.

A knock came at the door.

"I'll get it," she murmured, moving from me.

Taking another one of the half a million (slightly exaggerated) opportunities I'd taken since I'd donned my dress, I turned and looked into a mirror.

It had all come together perfectly.

I was Daisy but Daisy did her wedding just a little bit differently seeing as it was the day she was going to become Mrs. Marcus Sloan.

That meant my hair was teased full at the top back, but the sides had three soft twists in them, pulling them back to a big, swirly bun that nearly took up the entire back of my head. There was a diamanté comb tucked in one side (a girl's gotta have her sparkle, especially on her wedding day) and tendrils dangling around my ears. My bangs were full and brushed my brows.

I'd given up the smoke, the makeup girl bestowing on me subtle contouring, cheeks in pink, eyes in creams, browns, and pinks with magnificent shading and a set of fake eyelashes that I'd memorized the brand and style because they said perfection with a *kapow!*

My hair was romantically fabulous.

My makeup was understatedly dramatic.

My dress was d-i-v-i-n-e, *divine*.

It was white because I might not be a virgin but I was still a good girl and I reckoned I'd earned white, one way or another.

The bodice was a V-neck that went low (I might be going romantic for my Marcus but I was still Daisy, so if cleavage could be had, and I was a woman who could have a lot of it, it was had—and it *was*).

The whole top was made of lace, but the part from the built-in bustier over my shoulders, the lace was see-through. I had a rhinestone belt that was thin and pretty and made my waist look teeny-tiny. And the skirt flowed down in huge, soft, angelic, slanted vertical gossamer ruffles with a nice train at the back.

My wedding flowers (you could probably guess) were big cream gerbera daisies with little black buttons in the middle mixed with some cream roses, and subtle pretty pink velvet ribbons were bunched under the petals of the blooms so you could just catch a touch of their color.

I had the diamond earrings Marcus gave me the night I officially moved in with him in my ears. They looked like a passel of daises, so big they had to drop down in loop after loop. I also had the diamond bracelet on my wrist he gave me just because.

And of course, I had on the huge-ass diamond solitaire ring he gave me when he asked me to marry him.

He'd gone ostentatious with the engagement ring.

My man knew me well.

I'd picked a fluffy, wide, lacy blue garter for my blue and it was already on my thigh.

The dress and shoes (platform pumps with peek-a-boo toes covered in lace, with lace crawling up the back of my heel, a lace rosette at the toe with rhinestones in the middle, and high heels covered in diamanté—again, I was *Daisy*) were my new.

I had a lacy handkerchief that LaTeesha had given me stuffed in my cleavage that had been her grandmother's. That was my old.

And my borrowed I'd been in a panic about until I saw the pearly pink fingernail polish that Michelle brought and had shown me that morning. I'd loved it so I immediately replaced the one I'd picked because hers was way more perfect.

I was set.

Like I said.

Perfect.

"You can't see her," I heard Michelle say at the door.

"Honey, I'm walking her down to the restaurant," Marcus replied and I craned my neck to see down the hall in an effort to catch a glimpse of my man.

But Michelle had the door mostly closed, her rounded body in its pretty, pink bridesmaid dress wedged in the part that wasn't.

"You're meeting her at the door and walking her *in*," Michelle returned.

"Will you just let me see my wife?" Marcus asked on a sigh.

His wife.

Oh my.

"She isn't your wife yet and seeing her before the ceremony is bad luck! Heck, walking her *to* the ceremony is bad luck even if it starts at the restaurant doors! I don't know how I agreed to this. Like I told you two dozen times, you should let Doug give her away."

Michelle was freaking out.

And she was super sweet, if right now acting a little crazy. I'd thought that (except the crazy part) since I'd first laid eyes on her (okay, maybe the crazy part too).

I shouldn't have been surprised she'd be sweet. But since the day I met her months ago, I'd thought the same.

Partly because she took one look at me, burst into tears, and shouted, "You're perfect!"

But mostly because she helped make my man all the man he was.

And that man was a lot.

"We've had enough bad luck, every one of us," Marcus growled, and I watched him push in the door, doing this looking down at his sister who had his hair, but she had warm brown eyes. "No god there is would give a single one of us more."

Boy, I sure hoped that was the truth.

But I did it holding my breath.

Because Marcus looked fine all the time, in clothes, but especially out of them.

Though in a tux?

My coochie quivered.

Marcus was sauntering purposefully in the room, but the second he turned his head from his sister to me, he stopped dead.

"Hey, honey bunches of love," I called.

He said nothing.

His face was slack with wonder as he stared at me.

God, I loved my man.

I swirled my skirt side to side with a sway of my hips. "I take it you like it."

"Leave us," Marcus ordered his sister curtly.

I stared.

He might get exasperated with his sister's sweet brand of crazy, but he never talked to her like that.

"Marcus!" Michelle cried in shocked surprise.

See?

He twisted at the waist to look back at his sister. "Don't make me shove my own sister out of a suite in a fucking five-star hotel."

"Your language!" she yelled. "I thank God you had the control to curb it in front of the kids." She looked at me. "And he did. But *barely.*"

I giggled.

"Michelle," he warned.

"God, you're annoying," she snapped.

She also gave me a look that included a roll of her eyes right before she left.

But when she did, I panicked.

Because what I knew would happen, happened.

The minute the door clicked, Marcus stalked to me.

I lifted a hand his way, grabbed hold of the back of my skirts with the other one, and retreated, warning, "Don't you be messin' up my face and hair, sugar. We got us a fancy photographer and I'm gonna be picture perfect, not have sex hair!"

"You take one more step away from me, darling, I'll guarantee sex hair."

I halted.

Marcus got close.

"Christ, how can you get more beautiful?" he asked when he stopped, looking me up and down.

I planted my raised hand in his chest, shoved (ineffectually, I'll note), and hissed, "Now you're gonna make me cry."

"Yes, I am," he declared. "But the makeup girl is outside. I stopped her from leaving so she can fix it if she needs to."

"I don't have time to cry and have a makeup fix," I returned. "We're gettin' married in ten minutes."

"Daisy, honey, I hired out the entire restaurant. The only guests they have are you, me, Doug, and Michelle. They're good to wait."

Well then.

"I don't want a red face and puffy eyes in my wedding photos," I tried.

"You won't care."

"Yes, I will."

"No you won't."

"Yes I will!"

"Baby, every time you see it, you'll remember the day you married me was also the day I returned these."

And with that, he lifted his hand between us and from it dropped a necklace with a dainty gold chain and thirteen perfect pearls at the bottom. The biggest one in the middle, they got smaller but no less beautiful up the sides.

I'd know that necklace anywhere, if I'd seen it the day after I'd hocked it or if I saw it when I was old, addled, and a hundred-and-three.

My entire body seized.

Marcus moved behind me.

I felt the coolness of pearls and the tickle of a dainty gold chain at my neck.

Then I felt his lips at my ear.

"You thought Miss Annamae wanted you to get married wearing these pearls. And Miss Annamae helped make you the you for me. So you're getting married in these pearls."

He killed me, every time so softly, the fall felt like hitting a cloud.

"How—?" I started.

He kissed my neck and then wrapped his arms around me from behind.

"Your life starts now," he said all gentle and still in my ear. "The one you're meant to be leading. The one you've always deserved. I thought it best to mark that occasion in a way you'd never forget."

I twisted my neck to look at his handsome face.

"I would never have forgotten, sugar."

"It's my job to be sure."

God.

Marcus Sloan.

"I love you so much, I don't even know what to do with all of it," I whispered.

"I'm thrilled someone else understands that feeling."

God.

Marcus Sloan.

The tear lingered but finally traced down my cheek.

Marcus leaned in and caught it with his lips.

My belly fluttered, my heart clenched, and my hands went to his at my middle.

He lifted away and looked at me. "That all you got?"

"For now."

"Want to go get married?"

I nodded.

Fast.

And smiled.

It was shaky but it was big.

He smiled back at me, came around, took my hand, and tucked it into the crook of his arm.

He stopped long enough to offer me my bouquet and take hold of Michelle's to give to her.

Then he led me out of the room.

I held it together until I walked into the restaurant of the hotel that Marcus had hired out because it had two stories of windows and an unencumbered view of the mountains of Aspen covered in snow. We were going to be married in front of them. Then we were going to have a five-course meal in front of a blazing fire, all alone, the only guests in a beautiful, cozy, five-star restaurant in a beautiful, cozy five-star hotel.

After that, Doug and Michelle were going back to the suite, Marcus and I were spending our wedding night at his (no, *our*) place in Aspen, and tomorrow we were going to fly to the Maldives.

When I lost it, I didn't lose it because of the view.

I also didn't lose it because the big sprays of gerbera daisies and roses with their pink velvet ribbons that stood on columns that floated up from diaphanous sheers of white that would be what Marcus and I would stand between to get married (and stand around to have pictures taken by our fancy-ass photographer) were exactly what Michelle said they were when she'd checked on them after they'd been delivered.

That being perfect.

I didn't lose it because the fullness of Marcus getting me Miss Annamae's pearls back finally hit me.

And I didn't lose it because I felt beautiful, looked beautiful, and the beautiful man whose arm I was holding on to was about to become my husband.

I lost it because our small wedding party had an unexpected guest.

He looked older. I actually barely recognized him, especially looking stiff and uncomfortable in a suit.

But when Marcus and I hit the doors to the restaurant with Michelle trailing and Doug got up from his chair, looking at me with his mouth hanging open, and that man turned his eyes to me and they immediately got wet, I knew.

I knew he was a man called Stretch.

* * * *

"Daisy, darling, wake up."

I moved, blinked, opened my eyes, and from where my head was resting on Marcus's shoulder, I looked drowsily out the windows of our limousine.

It was dark. No streetlights. No overhead lights in a garage.

Just what seemed to be shadowed trees.

We were just back from our honeymoon.

The honeymoon was fab-you-*las*.

The return flight was killer.

I lifted my head and asked, "Where are we?"

"Home."

I looked to him. "Honey bunches of oats, this ain't no underground parking."

Eyes twinkling even in the dark car, he smiled.

Ronald did a sweep with the limo before he stopped and muted light came into the car.

Marcus's smile changed in a way I felt in my belly.

I stared at it and whispered, "What'd you do?"

I heard Ronald's door open.

Marcus took my hand.

But he didn't answer.

"What'd you do?" I repeated.

Ronald opened Marcus's door.

This Ronald didn't do. Unless otherwise instructed, Ronald opened my door first if I was in the car.

Marcus slid out and pulled me with him.

My platforms hit gravel.

My eyes hit light.

And my mouth dropped open.

Because in front of me, amongst a dark backdrop of not-quite-fledgling trees, stood a huge castle.

Yes.

A *castle*.

Just like it had been brought stone by stone straight from Germany or England or something.

It stood strong, high and proud, with turrets and everything.

Lit up totally with lights, I saw every inch.

Even the drawbridge.

And the moat.

Marcus's arm slid around my waist, curling my front into his side, and his lips found my ear.

"Welcome home, Daisy."

Well, apparently, way back when, I *did* blather on about my castles.

So Marcus built one for me.

My body bucked.

The sob sounded painful.

But it was the most beautiful pain I'd ever experienced.

And it was the pain of knowing I'd never really needed a castle.

I just needed my prince charming.

And I'd found him.

* * * *

"They'll be fine right there."

"You should wear them."

"They'll be fine *right there*, honey bunch."

Marcus turned me so my eyes left the glass-covered case with its ice-blue silk amongst which the circle of an add-a-pearl necklace was perfectly placed. A case that was standing displayed on a slant on the shelf that was above the seven-drawer jewelry cabinet in our walk-in closet.

The only other thing on that shelf was a fabulous wedding picture with a beautiful bride, a handsome groom, and three other dolled-up people, everyone smiling big, standing amongst daisies with a backdrop of mountains covered in glistening white snow.

The bride and groom were holding each other.

They were also holding glasses filled with champagne and etched with peacocks.

I looked up into my husband's eyes.

"Is there something you aren't telling me?" he asked gently.

"I want them perfect for her when she comes to us and it's time to give them to her," I replied.

I knew Marcus got it.

Because he always got it.

And because his smile took my breath away.

* * * *

Marcus

A number of years later...

"Darling, would you like to share with me what's troubling you?"

Marcus had his eyes on his wife.

Since they'd come home from the party, she'd been subdued.

She didn't normally come home from a Rock Chick party or after having anything to do with the Rock Chicks subdued.

She could come home drunk. She could come home exhausted from dancing in a club mostly populated by gay men. She could come home sharing she'd tipped a number of drag queens (or strippers) so many fifty dollar bills, he was out thousands. She could come home having used one of her (seven) stun guns. She could come home to an angry and/or alarmed husband because she'd been shot at or in a car chase.

This was the life of a Rock Chick.

Which meant he led the beleaguered life of the man of a Rock Chick.

As insane as it was, he wouldn't have it any other way. The women she'd found and formed into her posse were the best he'd ever met.

And they loved his wife down to their souls and made her happy.

"Nothin', darlin'," she murmured, turning toward the stairs. "I'm thinkin' tonight's a facial night."

He caught her as she would pass him and pulled her in his arms.

She looked up into his eyes.

"Tell me what's troubling you."

"Nothin' is, sugar."

"Then what's on your mind?"

"Ally's pregnant."

His chin jerked into his neck. "Christ. Those people breed like rabbits. How many is this?"

"Lee and Indy, two. Eddie and Jet, three. Hank and Roxie, two. Vance and Jules, three. Ava and Luke, two. Stella and Mace, one. Sadie and Hector, two. Ren and Ally, this will be two. Which makes almost seventeen."

Marcus had gone still.

She had them counted out.

Seventeen for her girls.

None for Daisy.

Marcus and his wife had everything.

But they couldn't have kids.

They'd tried.

But according to the doctors, and after two failed tries at in vitro, they'd been told it most likely just wasn't going to happen.

"Baby," he whispered.

"I'm fine," she lied.

He held her closer and dipped his face to hers.

"I'll say it again, and I really want you to think on it this time. We can adopt. Now, especially, we can adopt."

He'd taken all of his concerns legitimate and gone into business with Vito Zano's nephew, Daisy's friend Ally's husband, Ren Zano. There was nothing preventing them from adopting. Not their ages. Not money. Not his business. Not now.

She nodded. "I'll think on it, Marcus." Her eyes focused on his. "I'm real happy for her, sugar. Just—"

"I know," he said quietly, and fuck him, but he did know, and he hated knowing it. He bent to give her a soft kiss. "Go do your facial, darling. I'll bring some champagne up."

She gave him a distracted smile.

He let her go and watched her walk up the stairs.

Maybe he shouldn't have pushed it, seeing her before their wedding in her gown. Maybe he'd given them bad luck.

Or maybe there was a god, theirs, who wanted them to remember not to take anything for granted.

But he suspected there was a god, his, who wanted to use the most important thing in his life to remind him, to have the life he'd been able to give her, there was penance to be paid.

He'd done all he'd done and, especially when it allowed him to give Daisy the life she deserved, he'd done it without remorse.

But Marcus stared at the stairs up which his wife had disappeared.

And for the first time in his life, repentance sliced through him like a blade.

* * * *

She moved on him, her hands trailing his abs, her eyes watching, her glides slow, her face languid, her bottom lip caught in her teeth.

Christ, she was beautiful.

Marcus put his hands to her hips, bucked and turned, taking her to her back, him over her, loving hearing her breathy gasp.

He lifted his head, moved inside, feeling her sleek, wet silkiness gorgeous and tight around him. He looked in her eyes, found her hand, and laced his fingers through hers.

"Love you, baby," she whispered, rounding his thighs with her legs and lifting her hips to take him deep.

He touched his nose to hers. "Love you too, Daisy."

Then he took her mouth, tightened his hand in hers, slid his other one between them, down, and found her.

She whimpered against his tongue.

Marcus went faster.

"Love you," he whispered against her lips.

"You too, Marcus."

He kept moving, faster, deeper, harder.

"Love you," he repeated.

Her fingers clenched his hand.

"Love…" her body jolted, "love you. So much. Love you, honey." On that, her neck arched back and she breathed, "God,

Marcus."

Her hand tensed in his, so hard it caused pain through the webbing.

He didn't care.

He was focused on watching his wife coming.

* * * *

The next morning...

Marcus took in a breath then took hold of the case holding a pearl necklace against a bed of blue silk.

He took it to his pajama drawer, shoved the clothing aside, laid it on the bottom of the drawer and pulled the clothing over it.

After that, he went downstairs and nabbed the two glasses with peacocks on them that his wife had on display in a glass-fronted cupboard, the only things on their shelf.

He took them upstairs to their closet and set them where the pearls had been.

In the coming days, weeks, months, he knew she'd noticed the pearls were gone.

And it carved right through his heart what it meant when she didn't say a thing.

But his Daisy knew how to do one thing very well.

She knew how to move on.

And Marcus was put on this earth to do one thing and do it well.

To help her to get to that, if the need arose, and then be at her side when she did it.

* * * *

Two and a half months after that morning...

The door opened and Ren, sitting in a chair in front of Marcus's desk, turned his head to it.

He went still at what he saw.

Marcus looked that way.

And he went solid.

A second later, he forced himself to stand.

So did Ren.

"Hey, Ren," Daisy said and she walked in.

"Daisy," Ren replied. "You okay?"

Marcus was rounding his desk.

"Uh, yeah. Can I...sorry to interrupt. But can I have a second with my husband?" she asked, moving into the room.

"Of course," Ren murmured.

Marcus vaguely felt his partner's gaze, but only vaguely.

His focus was on his wife.

He had his hands spanning her waist, heard the door close after Ren, and instantly asked, "Which Rock Chick?"

"Pardon?"

He stared at her face and repeated, "Which Rock Chick?"

Her brows drew together, her head (and mess of hair) tipped to the side, and she asked, "What're you talkin' about, sugar?"

"You look..." He shook his head. "I don't know how you look."

And he didn't.

Even with all the shenanigans of the Rock Chicks, Daisy had never looked like this.

And those shenanigans had all ended, even if Daisy now spent her days being PA to Ally Zano in her private investigations business. A business that was situated right across the hall from Marcus and Ren's so the men could (unobtrusively) keep an eye on their women.

"I don't know how I look either."

With the stunned expression etched in her face, he lost patience and growled, "What's going on?"

"Marcus," she said, but that was all she said.

"Daisy," he clipped out.

She put her hands to his chest and looked into his eyes.

"I just got back from the doctor."

Fuck.

Fuck.

Penance.

Fuck.

His fingers gripped her tight as the entirety of his chest contracted to the point it felt like it was going to implode.

His voice was hoarse and rough and not his own when he asked,

"Why were you at the doctor, darling?"

"I'm..."

She looked to his chin, his throat, his chest, and when she lifted her eyes to his, they were filled with tears.

Fuck!

"Pregnant," she finished.

Marcus again went solid.

"I...she doesn't..." She shook her head. "She doesn't know how it happened. But when I skipped one month, then two, I took seven pregnancy tests at home. They were all positive. So I went to her. And she confirmed it." She leaned into him. "Marcus, honey, I'm preg—"

She didn't finish because his mouth crushed down on hers.

When he ended the kiss, he cupped her head and shoved it in his chest.

"I'm takin' that as you bein' happy," she noted, her voice muffled against his shirt.

His voice was just gruff when he forced out, "Yes. I'm happy."

His wife wound her arms around his middle.

"I'm pregnant," she whispered into his chest.

Marcus was breathing through his nose.

"I'm pregnant," she repeated.

Marcus closed his eyes as the wonder in her voice started coating the region around his heart.

He felt her push her head back.

And he also felt her hand on his jaw.

Last, he felt her thumb trail through the line of wet that was on his cheek.

He opened his eyes and saw her gazing up at him, her blue eyes lit with happy.

"We're pregnant, baby," she whispered.

Then her body bucked and she let out a sob that ended in a peal of laughter that filled his office with bells.

Only then did Marcus smile.

* * * *

Six and a half months later...

Marcus walked into the room.

"*Well?*" Tex boomed.

He looked at the big man with his big beard and wild head of gray-blond hair in his plaid flannel shirt, and then his eyes swept through the room.

It was so full, some were coming up from sitting on the floor.

"God, tell us, brother," Duke demanded, and Marcus locked eyes with the man with the gray braid, leather vest, black T-shirt, and red bandana wrapped around his head.

"Serious, dude, spill!" a man (loosely termed as thus) who called himself The Kevster shouted. He was standing but doing it shifting foot to foot.

"It's a girl," Marcus said. His eyes moved to one of the women in the room. "Her name is Annamae Shirleen."

Delivering that, he watched as tears slid down Shirleen's cheeks.

Marcus looked through the Rock Chicks, their men, and the rest of Daisy's friends that were family and finished, "Both mother and daughter are perfect."

"Holy crap," Indy breathed then burst into tears and shoved her face in Lee's chest.

"Oh my God," Jet murmured then smiled a smile that made a very pretty woman stunning, turning to aim it to her husband, Eddie.

"Holy cow," Roxie whispered, then she too burst into tears as well as shoved her face in her husband, Hank's, chest.

"Damn," Jules muttered though a huge smile, and leaned against her husband, Vance.

"Awesome," Ava sighed, her body visibly trembling from either trying not to cry, or perhaps laugh, so her husband Luke pulled her closer.

"Lordy be," Stella mumbled, also smiling, standing in the round of her husband, Mace's arm.

"Aces," Sadie breathed, tears brimming, and her husband, Hector, pulled her into a tight embrace.

Shirleen just stood in the curve of her adopted son, Roam's arm, silently weeping.

"Righteous," Ally muttered, looking like she was about ready to burst out laughing. She had both her arms wrapped around an equally smiling Ren's middle and she gave him a visible squeeze.

"Cigars, all around!" a woman named Annette declared loudly, opening a big macramé bag and pulling out a fistful of brightly-colored, plastic-covered cigars made of bubble gum.

"Oh my God," Tod mumbled and turned to his husband, Stevie. "Thank heaven I went with the pink baby book. I know the ultrasound said girl, but sometimes they mess that up. I was thinking yellow, just to be sure. But Daisy screams *pink!* Seeing as I already filled it with seven-dozen pictures of her pregnant, and seven dozen more of that shower May threw her, I can't go back now. I'm glad in twenty years I don't have to explain a pink baby book to a surprise boy."

Stevie just shook his head at his husband, but he did it smiling.

"*Rock 'n' roll!*" Tex bellowed for some reason, making some jump, others smile, and the rest start laughing. "Can we see her?" he asked. "That bein' both *hers*," he clarified. "Daisy and Mini-Daisy?"

Marcus nodded but said, "She wants Shirleen first."

He nearly had to jump out of the way as Shirleen sprinted to the doors behind him.

Sniff, Shrileen's other adopted son, chuckled.

"Woman's nuts for babies," he muttered.

"Thank God," Ava mumbled into Luke's chest.

Marcus let his gaze slide through the Rock Chicks. "She'll want the lot of you next."

He got nods and then Marcus looked to Darius. He looked to Lee. After that, he looked to Luke.

He felt Michelle come up to his side. His sister gave him a hug.

He hugged her back and said into her ear, "Be ready. We need to take turns, but she wants you too."

He lifted his head and looked down at his sister in time to catch her nod and witness her wet cheeks before a smiling-so-big-his-face-had-to-hurt Doug pulled her from Marcus's arms into his own.

Before he turned to retrace his steps, he looked at two last people.

"She wants the both of you too."

Smithie's smile split his face, he grabbed LaTeesha's hand, and they followed Marcus as he led them to his wife.

And their baby daughter.

* * * *

Daisy

Five days later…

"You know what?" I asked Marcus.

He was across from me in our bed. His body on his side, his legs curved up, his knees touching mine because I was in the same position, mirrored opposite him.

Annamae lay sleeping in her swaddles between us.

His beautiful blue eyes came from the top of her dark fuzzed head to me.

"What, honey?" he asked.

"She never has to do it."

He took his hand from our baby girl's belly, reached out, and ran the tips of his fingers down my cheekbone.

"Do what, darling?" he whispered.

"She'll never have to build castles."

That was when his hand curved around the back of my head and he pulled me across the pillows until the tops of our heads collided, our eyes aimed at baby fuzz.

"Never," he said, his voice gruff.

"Not ever," I whispered.

Finding his hand and linking it with mine, I held it at the bottom of her swaddled feet against the sheets on the bed where we'd made our Annamae.

Me and my prince charming in our castle with our happily ever after swaddled and sleeping between a momma who loved her, a daddy who adored her, born into a world that just with that, she had everything.

* * * *

Thirteen years later...

"A Southern woman always has her table laid."

"Yes, Momma."

I took my eyes from my daughter as I saw a flash go across the doorway to the dining room.

A flash of a dark head on top of a tall, lean eleven-year-old body.

"Smithson Sloan!" I called. "What'd I say about runnin' in the house?"

Marcus sauntered in the doorway and stopped.

He winked at his girl.

He grinned at me.

"Your son doesn't listen to his mother," I declared.

"Stretch!" he bellowed. "You best be listening to your mother."

"Right, Dad!" Stretch shouted from somewhere, probably making trouble, and definitely lying.

Shouting in my house.

I rolled my eyes to the ceiling.

Annamae giggled and it sounded like bells.

I rolled my eyes to my girl.

I loved that sound.

Even so.

"This isn't funny, honey bunches of oats," I told her.

"It's hilarious, Momma," she replied, her finger in her necklace, not twisting, just looping around.

My girl loved her pearls.

I knew this because she'd worn them every day since the day her daddy and I gave them to her.

Marcus came into the room, took his daughter in the curve of his arm, and kissed the top of her head.

Having done that, he looked to me.

"Are you cooking or am I?" he asked.

Had he lost his mind?

What kind of question was that?

"Whose house is this?" I asked back.

"Ours," he answered.

Okay, he was right about that.

"Whose kitchen is it?" I went on.

He grinned and pulled his baby girl closer. "Yours."

"Then who's cooking?"

"Darling, get on with it. Your family's hungry."

"I'm givin' Southern woman lessons to my daughter, *comprende?*"

"She gives them to me, like, every day," Annamae whispered to her daddy.

"I don't want you to forget," I shot at her.

"Momma, if a boy doesn't open my door for me, Daddy'll break his legs and Stretch'll shoot him. You got nothing to worry about." Her grin got cheeky as she concluded, "*Comprende?*"

I *comprende*'d because that was probably the sorry truth.

My son needed to stop hanging with the Hot Bunch and their crazy posse. He was better at target practice than Vance, something Vance shared with me proudly.

Something that gave me heart palpitations.

I didn't even think of what Stella told me that Mace told her that he'd taught him to do, and Mace didn't even live in Denver anymore. He'd taught him over Skype, of all things.

And I'd had to have a facial *and* call my masseuse when Stretch came back after spending an afternoon with Tex.

To communicate my feelings on the matter, I huffed.

"You gonna help your momma cook?" I asked my girl.

"Yep."

"Then get your behind in the kitchen, sugar."

She grinned at me again, looked up at her daddy, and grinned at him and got a kiss on the nose for her troubles.

I felt that in my belly.

And right in the heart.

Annamae took off from the room, my husband watched her, and when she disappeared, his eyes came to me.

"You do know our daughter has a huge ole crush on Callum Nightingale," I shared.

His face turned thunderous.

Uh-oh.

Right, time to fix that.

Easy.

"Love you," I whispered.

The thunder went out of his face.

"Love you too," Marcus whispered back.

"Walk me to the kitchen, sugar?"

He lifted his arm to me.

I rounded my grand dining table set with the finest china, crystal, and silver that I could find.

I took my husband's arm.

And he escorted me to the kitchen.

We barely crossed over the threshold when Stretch shouted from somewhere not close, not far, "I want Las Delicias!"

My boy, shouting in the house and dissin' his momma's cooking.

I glared murder at Marcus.

My husband just burst out laughing.

Sign up for the 1001 Dark Nights Newsletter
and be entered to win a Tiffany Key necklace.

There's a contest every month!

Go to www.1001DarkNights.com to subscribe

As a bonus, all subscribers will receive a free
1001 Dark Nights story
The First Night
by Lexi Blake & M.J. Rose

Turn the page for a full list of the
1001 Dark Nights fabulous novellas...

Discover 1001 Dark Nights Collection Three

HIDDEN INK by Carrie Ann Ryan
A Montgomery Ink Novella

BLOOD ON THE BAYOU by Heather Graham
A Cafferty & Quinn Novella

SEARCHING FOR MINE by Jennifer Probst
A Searching For Novella

DANCE OF DESIRE by Christopher Rice

ROUGH RHYTHM by Tessa Bailey
A Made In Jersey Novella

DEVOTED by Lexi Blake
A Masters and Mercenaries Novella

Z by Larissa Ione
A Demonica Underworld Novella

FALLING UNDER YOU by Laurelin Paige
A Fixed Trilogy Novella

EASY FOR KEEPS by Kristen Proby
A Boudreaux Novella

UNCHAINED by Elisabeth Naughton
An Eternal Guardians Novella

HARD TO SERVE by Laura Kaye
A Hard Ink Novella

DRAGON FEVER by Donna Grant
A Dark Kings Novella

KAYDEN/SIMON by Alexandra Ivy/Laura Wright
A Bayou Heat Novella

STRUNG UP by Lorelei James
A Blacktop Cowboys® Novella

MIDNIGHT UNTAMED by Lara Adrian
A Midnight Breed Novella

TRICKED by Rebecca Zanetti
A Dark Protectors Novella

DIRTY WICKED by Shayla Black
A Wicked Lovers Novella

A SEDUCTIVE INVITATION by Lauren Blakely
A Seductive Nights New York Novella

SWEET SURRENDER by Liliana Hart
A MacKenzie Family Novella

Go to www.1001DarkNights.com for more information.

Discover 1001 Dark Nights Collection One

FOREVER WICKED by Shayla Black
CRIMSON TWILIGHT by Heather Graham
CAPTURED IN SURRENDER by Liliana Hart
SILENT BITE: A SCANGUARDS WEDDING by Tina Folsom
DUNGEON GAMES by Lexi Blake
AZAGOTH by Larissa Ione
NEED YOU NOW by Lisa Renee Jones
SHOW ME, BABY by Cherise Sinclair
ROPED IN by Lorelei James
TEMPTED BY MIDNIGHT by Lara Adrian
THE FLAME by Christopher Rice
CARESS OF DARKNESS by Julie Kenner

Also from 1001 Dark Nights

TAME ME by J. Kenner

Go to www.1001DarkNights.com for more information.

Discover 1001 Dark Nights Collection Two

WICKED WOLF by Carrie Ann Ryan
WHEN IRISH EYES ARE HAUNTING by Heather Graham
EASY WITH YOU by Kristen Proby
MASTER OF FREEDOM by Cherise Sinclair
CARESS OF PLEASURE by Julie Kenner
ADORED by Lexi Blake
HADES by Larissa Ione
RAVAGED by Elisabeth Naughton
DREAM OF YOU by Jennifer L. Armentrout
STRIPPED DOWN by Lorelei James
RAGE/KILLIAN by Alexandra Ivy/Laura Wright
DRAGON KING by Donna Grant
PURE WICKED by Shayla Black
HARD AS STEEL by Laura Kaye
STROKE OF MIDNIGHT by Lara Adrian
ALL HALLOWS EVE by Heather Graham
KISS THE FLAME by Christopher Rice
DARING HER LOVE by Melissa Foster
TEASED by Rebecca Zanetti
THE PROMISE OF SURRENDER by Liliana Hart

Also from 1001 Dark Nights

THE SURRENDER GATE By Christopher Rice
SERVICING THE TARGET By Cherise Sinclair

Go to www.1001DarkNights.com for more information.

About Kristen Ashley

Kristen Ashley was born in Gary, Indiana, USA and nearly killed her mother and herself making it into the world, seeing as she had the umbilical cord wrapped around her neck (already attempting to accessorize and she hadn't taken her first breath!). Her mother said they took Kristen away, put her Mom back in her room, her mother looked out the window, and Gary was on fire (Dr. King had been assassinated four days before). Kristen's Mom remembered thinking it was the end of the world. Quite the dramatic beginning.

Nothing's changed.

Kristen grew up in Brownsburg, Indiana and has lived in Denver, Colorado and the West Country of England. Thus, she's blessed to have friends and family around the globe. Her family was (is) loopy (to say the least) but loopy is good when you want to write. They all lived together on a very small farm in a small farm town in the heartland. She grew up with Glenn Miller, The Everly Brothers, REO Speedwagon and Whitesnake (and the wardrobes that matched).

Needless to say, growing up in a house full of music, clothes and love was a good way to grow up.

And as she keeps growing, it keeps getting better.

You can find more information about her books at www.kristenashley.net.

The Deep End

The Honey Series
By Kristen Ashley
Coming March 7, 2017

Enter a decadent sensual world where gorgeous alpha males are committed to fulfilling a woman's every desire…

Olivier isn't sure what he's gotten himself into when he joins the Honey Club, only that a dark part of him hungers for the lifestyle offered by this exclusive club. Here, no boundary will be left untested…and one's deepest fantasies will become an exquisite reality.

When Amélie invites Olivier to surrender, she gives the alpha submissive what he craves. Soon they both find themselves falling harder than they ever anticipated—but as their connection deepens, the truth about Olivier's past could destroy everything…

Gripping and seductive, *The Deep End* is the first book in a sensational new series from bestselling author Kristen Ashley.

* * * *

That done, she walked right to the center of the room.

She turned to him and saw him automatically duck, as if the top of the frame of the door could not always be assumed would be one he wouldn't run right into.

It was a sight that made him even more alluring.

As he slowly closed the door behind him and moved his eyes to look through the room, taking it in, she watched them get wide.

They dropped to her and his amusement was clear. Not only radiating from his gaze but twitching at his lips.

Another unusual—and unacceptable—reaction.

He thought this was funny.

She hoped like fuck she had the opportunity to prove him wrong.

She crossed her arms on her chest and slightly put out a foot, like she was about to start tapping her toe. In the wrap dress she wore, she knew this opened the overlap, not exposing anything, but the promise for him was impossible to resist.

His attention dropped to her legs.

"In the playrooms," she began with a snap, and his gaze cut up to hers, "I want eye contact. Unless otherwise instructed, you should not only feel free to look me directly in the eyes, if I'm in your line of sight or I'm not giving you something that your body's natural reaction would make it difficult to meet my gaze, I require it."

She stood there staring as he did nothing but dip his chin in acknowledgment.

Cheeky.

Exceptionally cheeky.

Fabulous.

"Unless I've asked for their silence or for them to ask for leave to speak, I also require my toys to respond when they're spoken to. Even if it's only a 'yes, Mistress,' or 'no, Mistress.'"

His stance relaxed, like he was settling in at the beginning of a show he found vaguely intriguing, and his deep rumble of a voice bounced like boulders through the room. "Yes, Mistress."

Christ, even his voice declared his challenge.

"Excellent," she allowed. "Your name?"

"Olivier," he answered.

French.

Also unusual, at least in this country. And interesting.

She liked it a great deal.

She studied him.

He let her, holding her eyes.

"I'm Mistress Amélie," she eventually informed him.

"I know. You got a lotta fans out there . . . Mistress."

The hesitation over him saying "Mistress" gave less of the impression he was testing her and more of the *strange* impression the word was unpracticed when, with any experienced sub, it would slip right off their tongue.

She made no comment to that.

"There are things we should go over," she remarked.

"Right," he stated, his big body adjusting again, now like he was settling in further, intent on giving her the same attention he would a flight attendant who gave the safety address.

That being no more than a courtesy.

She fought the shiver his actions created but allowed the irritation.

"Your safe word is kitten," she stated.

"Yes, Mistress."

"You're open to any kind of play," she went on.

"Yes, Mistress."

"It's important and now's the time to share should there be anything you wish me to shy away from, Olivier. Especially as this is the first time I've played with you."

Something in his eyes flashed. Blue eyes that were the color of nothing and everything. Not sky. Not sea. Not midnight. A pure blue that only existed in the unchartable depths of a rainbow.

She felt that flash snake up between her thighs, taking residence in her womb.

He wanted this conversation done so she would play with him. He wanted the preliminaries over so they'd get to the good stuff.

He wanted her.

She stared into those blue eyes and for a moment felt mesmerized.

For God's sake, Leigh, she berated herself in an effort to pull it together. *Rainbow?*

"Olivier," she prompted.

"I'm open to anything," he confirmed.

She threw her hand out, indicating the padded vault, the displayed tack . . . the stall.

"Anything?" she pushed.

He held her gaze like a dare. "Anything." Again his lips twitched. "Mistress."

She quieted and took him in.

Aryas would not let a voyeur past the front door. Amélie fancied he'd paid secret spy guys like the gentleman in the Bond film who created all the devices that got James out of a bind to set up a force field that would instantly eject anyone who wished to use the Bee's Honey as a curiosity or to get their rocks off observing and not participating (thus not embracing the lifestyle). Certainly not someone who found the whole thing amusing.

"Am I amusing you?" she whispered, the whisper holding a tremor that was not of fear but of anger.

His face set hard and his two words were so firm, the boulders again came tumbling.

"Absolutely not."

"Then can you explain your humor?" she asked.

He shrugged. "Sure. You are un-fucking-believably beautiful. You're also un-fucking-believably hot. But I wouldn't guess with the acres that make all of you, every inch of it so damned sweet, you're a walking wet dream, that when you get riled you're also un-fucking-believably cute. And there is no way in fuck five minutes ago, you told me a gorgeous redhead was gonna lead me to a room and make me her pony, I would be cool with that. But standin' here with you, I'm totally fuckin' cool with that."

It took a good deal, and she expended every bit of effort she needed to accomplish it, but at his final two points, Amélie didn't blink.

Instead, she decided to finish this part up.

Immediately.

On behalf of 1001 Dark Nights,

Liz Berry and M.J. Rose would like to thank ~

Steve Berry
Doug Scofield
Kim Guidroz
Jillian Stein
InkSlinger PR
Dan Slater
Asha Hossain
Chris Graham
Pamela Jamison
Fedora Chen
Jessica Johns
Dylan Stockton
Richard Blake
BookTrib After Dark
and Simon Lipskar